Who Is He To You?

By: Bianca Harrison

"As my life flashes before my eyes,
I'm wondering will I ever see another
sunrise?
So just pull the trigger..."
-Rihanna (Russian Roulette)

Book Dedication:

This book is dedicated to all the women of the world. We truly make things happen! A special dedication to, Pamela Turner, Sandra Bland, Breonna Taylor, Korryn Gaines, Atatiana Jefferson, Shantel Davis, and a host of others that have lost their lives due to police brutality. To all my QUEENS,

I love you!

Acknowledgements:

First, I give all praise to my awesome God, for blessing me with a gift of writing. I couldn't have done any of this without him. Thank you to my amazing kids, they keep me young. Next to my other half, my family, and friends that hold me down, book after book. A special shout-out to Renee at (Cover Me) for an awesome book cover, Megan at Joseph Editorial Services, doing what she does best (transforming gems into diamonds). I thank you both so much. As well as the book promoters, book clubs, and my supporters. A special shout-out to Ebony Evans and EyeCU Reading & Social Network for the free style Friday, that prompts this book! Man you guys' rock! The readers always want more and I had to give them just that. I appreciate the opportunity. I would love to hear what you guys think of this book, feedback and anything else. Please drop me a line at authorbiancaharrison@gmail.com.

CONTENTS

CHAPTER ONE 1

CHAPTER TWO 8

CHAPTER THREE 16

CHAPTER FOUR 24

CHAPTER FIVE 35

CHAPTER SIX 41

CHAPTER SEVEN 50

CHAPTER EIGHT 62

CHAPTER NINE 70

CHAPTER TEN 81

CHAPTER ELEVEN 87

CHAPTER TWELVE 100

CHAPTER THIRTEEN 108

CHAPTER FOURTEEN 120

CHAPTER FIFTEEN 131

CHAPTER SIXTEEN 145

CHAPTER SEVENTEEN 150

CHAPTER EIGHTEEN 155

CHAPTER NINETEEN 168

CHAPTER TWENTY 183

CHAPTER TWENTY-ONE 200

CHAPTER TWENTY-TWO 215

CHAPTER TWENTY-THREE 223

CHAPTER TWENTY-FOUR 235

CHAPTER TWENTY-FIVE 244

CHAPTER TWENTY-SIX 250

CHAPTER TWENTY-SEVEN 255

CHAPTER TWENTY-EIGHT 268

THE AFTERMATH 278

THE END 283

What Is Domestic Violence? 284

CHAPTER ONE

"**S**teve, thanks for dinner. I'll get back with you as soon as possible with a proposal," Val said. Steve was an executive at a top firm in Atlanta, who invited Bird and Val to dinner, along with his wife and other colleagues.

"I'm glad you accepted my invite and you all were able to join us," he replied, as he stood up to pull out Val's chair.

At the same time, Bird stood up. "I got it," he said, with a stern tone.

As awkward as it was, Bird made it difficult to enjoy dinner. He squeezed Val's leg if he thought she was too chummy with the fellas.

As soon as dinner was over, they rushed out of Ruth Chris Steakhouse like they had to be somewhere. Bird didn't open the restaurant door for Val as they exited, nor did he say a word as they got to the car.

There was silence on the way home. Val needed to make a pit stop, but declined to speak because she didn't know what mood Bird was in. That dinner meant a lot to her and her company but bringing Bird along wasn't a good idea. He behaves well when others didn't pose a threat to him. He drove the long way home and didn't utter a word. Val turned the volume up on the radio, so that it wouldn't be so awkward. Thirty minutes later, they pulled into the driveway of their nice size home in a predominantly white neighborhood. Their lifestyle wasn't lavish, but they worked hard to get the things they had. He pressed the remote for the garage to open. Val couldn't wait to get in the house, to take off her heels. Once the car was turned off, Val immediately opened the door.

"Close the damn door!" Bird said.

Val looked confused but did as she was told. "What is it?"

"I noticed how Steve was flirting with you when I turned my head. He knew way too much of our personal business and had the audacity to ask me about my son! How fucking stupid could you be, Val? I haven't seen my son in years and you are with these uppity motherfuckers telling my business, how dare you, BITCH!"

WHO IS HE TO YOU?

"Bird, I'm sorry! It wasn't like that. Steve wasn't flirting with me and I only mentioned Tyler, when he asked me about kids."

WHACK! Val's head hit the dashboard. Her head slung back quickly from the force. She immediately put one hand over her head, looking over at Bird in tears.

"I said I was sorry!" she screamed. "You didn't give me an opportunity to explain!"

"Nothing to explain, when he's asking me about my son and had no business knowing that. Too much information, Val! Get your ass in the house and fix your face. I'll be up shortly and I expect you to be naked!" he demanded.

Val was in disbelief once again. She'd thought an evening out would be just what they needed. She understood Bird was stressed out about Chanel ripping his son away from him, not hearing from her in years or their whereabouts, but it was no reason for him to hit her. Val made a mistake and wished Steve would have kept his mouth shut. Val did as she was told, which was get out the car, with one hand placed on her forehead. She looked back, as Bird sat in the car with his cell phone placed to his ear. Val then let herself into their home. She looked around before heading to the bedroom. Once there, she took a look at her forehead and noticed a huge bruised knot, not knowing how she would cover it up for work tomorrow. A tear fell from her eyes, as she sucked it up to get ready for bed.

A half an hour later, Bird came into the bedroom and stripped butt naked. Val had showered and climbed in bed already, she was exhausted and not in the mood for sex. She had her gown on, not following through with Bird's request to be naked. He placed his phone on the nightstand and then climbed in bed, rubbing on Val, noticing she was fully clothed. He looked at her wondering why she didn't do as she was told.

"I know you not wearing that to bed? How are we supposed to fuck with that on?" he asked, looking at her gown.

"Baby, I'm not in the mood. My head hurts and I'm exhausted. I'll take care of you tomorrow."

"Like hell you will! You owe me, for running your mouth and mentioning my son to that punk at that dinner table!"

Bird started fondling Val. She didn't budge; he was draining her.

WHO IS HE TO YOU?

"Baby, I said I'm sorry. Please let me make it up to you tomorrow," she pleaded.

By that time, he started kissing on her neck, down to her breast. Val tried to push Bird off her. He then placed his hands on her vagina and realized she also had panties on. Bird looked at Val and shook his head. He sat up hovering over her and then ripped her panties and then proceeded to do the same with her gown. "I told you to take this shit off!"

"Please, Bird my head hurts," Val pleaded.

"My dick hurts, so what?"

Bird proceeded to enter Val without her consent as she laid there in tears. Val tried to push him off of her, but Bird was too much. He thrust inside of her as he felt her come alive. Bird tried to tongue kiss Val, but she turned her head, only for him to grab her by the face and force his tongue in her mouth.

"Fuck me, Val," he insisted.

Val sniffed, wiped her tears and then gave in. She knew it wasn't a battle to fight, so she figured, if she fucked Bird, he would roll over and go to sleep. Val rolled over on top of Bird and sat on his no good dick.

She slow motioned on him, pulled him to sit up, while she grinded on him, making love to a man who just forced himself inside of her. Val then glided off of him and proceeded to put her mouth on his dick. Bird moaned in excitement, as he pushed Val's head up and down. She sucked the tip of his dick and sucked his balls until he motioned for her to get up and get on all fours. Val knew Bird and hated when he entered her anally. She never had sex back there, until Bird forced himself in her, ripping her apart one night. She remembered crying and being sore for days. As he entered her from the back, it got a little better, but she didn't enjoy it and she couldn't tell him no. He would do it anyway.

Bird oiled his dick and her anus, and then proceeded to enter her slowly in the asshole. She still cringed and couldn't wait until it was over. He humped and humped, gliding in and out of her ass, watching himself in the mirror.

"Val, baby."I'm so sorry for hitting you. Sometimes my anger gets the best of me and I end up taking it out on you. I love you, so much. You do know that right?" Bird said, as he grinded inside of Val.

"It's okay, sweetheart. I'm sorry as well, for anything I've done to get you to that point. I know you love me and I love you too."

WHO IS HE TO YOU?

"Baby, I want you to cum with me," Bird said, about to climax.

Val threw it back a little harder, rotating her ass on his dick. She moaned and moaned, knowing good and well she wasn't cumming, but anything to speed up the process. She felt Bird thrust, as sweat race from his forehead onto her cheeks. He had climaxed. He slowly pulled out of her, slapping her on the ass. Val started to get up, but Bird ordered her to stay put.

"Sweetheart, lay back. I'm going to get a rag and come back to clean you up."

Val was uneasy and couldn't wait until Bird came back with a warm cloth. Once they both were wiped down, Bird climbed back into bed, as Val snuggled up against his chest. She didn't know if she was coming or going, he had her so whipped.

CHAPTER TWO

V al was in the office earlier than usual. She wanted to get there so she could close her door to show that she didn't want to be bothered and to hide the knot on her forehead. She sipped her usual white chocolate mocha latte from Starbucks, as she heard employees starting to arrive in the office. She was glad it was the weekend and planned on leaving the office early but had a conference call with a very important client.

Val looked at a picture on her desk of her and Bird, which was taken a few years ago. Bird was handsome. He was six feet, had almond shape eyes, a dark mocha complexion, fit for the most part, low fade cut, and the personality that could charm anyone. Bird was also a graduate from Georgia State University. He was a web designer and IT technician with a marketing firm in downtown Atlanta. He was smart and technically inclined. They met about seventeen years ago, while attending school in the same area, as Val was a Spelman graduate. She was a top executive at her firm. Val studied the picture as if she could get that Bird back. He was cool, down to earth, and always treated her like a queen. Bird today was still the same in many areas, but behind closed doors, he had another side to him.

Val knew all his issues stemmed from his past. He watched his father abuse the women in his life, even his mother. His mother finally got the nerve to fight back, but he'd told Val stories on how he shadowed his dad, who would teach he and his brother how a woman should be punished, if she ever got out of line. At least that's what he told Val during one of their therapy sessions in the past. She remembered the first time he'd hit her and she'd been trying to make it work ever since by making excuses, going to therapy, and doing what he asked of her. Hoping he would come around.

Thinking back, Val could still remember him slapping her across the face because the chicken she cooked was half done. After that, she got on YouTube and became the best cook ever. He also cheated on her with Chanel, who later became pregnant with their son, Tyler. Bird was back and forth between Val and Chanel and he thought it was okay. He also beat Chanel at times when he couldn't have his way. Val had been through it with Bird, but she still remained faithful because she knew God could turn anything around, as her great grandmother use to say.

It was the last straw for Chanel when Bird took their son out of school one day and threatened that she would never see him again, if she had their son around another nigga. Chanel had started dating again and Bird got word of it, then busted her lip when she came over to pick Tyler up. Val never got in the way of their relationship, she kind of stood in the background. But she loved Tyler like her own, since she couldn't seem to have any, due to Polycystic Ovarian Syndrome making it harder for her to get pregnant. Val knew one day; she would get the strength just like Chanel to just up and disappear.

Chanel took their son and left town, Bird was devastated, but if he could get his hands on Chanel, he would probably kill her.

Val heard a knock on her door and jumped. She turned her attention to the entrance, "Come in."

Emily walked in with a smile on her face as always. "Good morning, boss lady. Guess what?"

"What?"

"We got the b-i-d we got the b-i-d!" Emily said, as she twirled around the office.

WHO IS HE TO YOU?

"Baker & Connor? Hot damn! That's awesome! I knew you could do it!" Val responded, standing up to give Emily a high five.

"Yes, Shantel emailed me last night, after I emailed you that report for your conference call today. I wasn't going to bother you last night."

"That's awesome girl. I owe you lunch."

"Hey what's all the racket about?" Derrick asked, walking inside Val's office.

"Emily just scored big time!" Val conceded.

"Whatever it is, I know it was big," Derrick said digging in a bag he was carrying. "I brought biscuits for everyone, just wanted to see if you two would like one?"

"No thank you, I'm good. I just had my usual, but I appreciate it so much," Val responded.

"Yes, give me whatever you got! I am starving," Emily said.

Derrick handed Emily a biscuit and smiled. He looked at Val, "Are you sure?" He then paused, "How did you get that knot on your forehead?"

"Yes, I'm sure," Val said as she tried to find an excuse, in response to Derrick. "I was reading a text and walked straight into the end of the door. I noticed it this morning, but guess I failed at covering it up."

Emily looked at Val's forehead and shook her head. "Girl that door is becoming something serious."

"Glad that's all it was. I'll talk to you ladies later," Derrick said, and exited, closing the door behind him.

"While I was working on that bid, you were getting beat on, again?" Emily asked, concerned.

Val looked at Emily, as it was none of her business. Emily was the only person at work Val confided in, since they were close. She hoped that Emily would keep her word and never tell a sole about the abuse she was receiving at home.

"Emily, it wasn't like that. I really did walk into the door this time. This is one time, Bird didn't…"

"Didn't what? You know damn well I'm not believing you walked into a door. It could be possible, but that bruise has Bird's name written all over it. He's beating you and cheating on you with ole girl downstairs! Now, he needs his ass beat!"

WHO IS HE TO YOU?

"Emily, what do you mean he's cheating on me? You never said anything to me about this, and who is ole girl downstairs?" Val asked, confused and pissed.

"I thought you knew! Come on, Val, you didn't have a clue about Tyra Buffin?"

Val was shocked. She looked at Emily weird, trying to figure out where she heard that name from. "Who else knows about this?"

"Several people have been whispering about it. I honestly thought you knew but didn't want to talk about it. She's Gail's assistant in the billing department. When Bird left your office last week, one of the girls said he was downstairs and brought her lunch in a hurry. That's fucked up, you didn't know and she's in the same building."

Val put her hand over her head. She was starting to get a headache. She was hurt and for the most part embarrassed. Once again, Bird had pulled a big one over her head. Val didn't know Tyra but heard her name a time or two.

"I'm sorry, Val. I don't want to get you upset and then go calling Bird, which may lead to him putting his hands on you again."

"That mother… I helped him get that girl a job, but I had no clue he was sleeping with her!" Val hollered, hitting her desk with her fist. "Ouch!"

"Wait a minute; you know this chic?" Emily asked, stunned.

"I don't know her personally, but apparently she got laid off from Bird's firm and was in need of a job. He asked me to see if we were hiring and to submit her résumé because she was good people. I spoke with Human Resources and now she's here. She's been here for about three months now. I guess that explains why he's always here, in the past he never cared to stop by the office."

"Valerie, that's fucked up. Excuse my French, but he's bold as fuck! I wonder if she knows about you. I'm very curious. She seems young, but like a very nice girl. I also wonder if she ever worked with Bird."

"Don't worry, I'll get to the bottom of it." Val looked at the clock.

"Sorry, I got a conference call and need to dial in."

Emily walked over and gave Val a hug. She knew her friend and colleague was hurt and felt bad that she didn't know. Val let go and watched Emily exit the office, then heard her phone going off. She looked at it and saw her mom calling but couldn't take the call. Her mind was in a thousand places and couldn't understand after all she's done for him, why wasn't she enough? Who was he to her? Val was smart but got herself in a fucked up situation. So many thoughts came to mind. *If she left, what would happen to the house, their rental properties, their lifestyle, their everything?* Although they weren't married, Val and Bird were doing married shit.

Bird had talked her into getting a rental property and setting up a bank account, that she put most of her pay in. And here she was, on the sideline, looking like a fool. She knew she needed answers, but at what cost? Val snapped out of her daze and immediately dialed into the conference. She needed to be focus because unlike some, she had to prove herself to her boss, Marc.

CHAPTER THREE

Val made it her business to go downstairs and talk to Gail. She usually stayed in her lane, but she wanted to see Tyra and what kind of competition she was up against. Val was a genuine and outgoing person, but she felt the need to make an appearance, since people were talking. Gail was on a call as Val stood in the doorway, so she decided to walk around and speak to everyone.

"How's it going, Tyra? Are you liking the job so far?" Val asked, as she was bold enough to approach Tyra's desk while others peeped over their cubbies.

"Hi there, Valerie, right?" she asked as if she didn't know who helped her get the job.

"Yes, Valerie or Val."

"It's going pretty good. Everyone here is great. I have no complaints."

"Awesome!"

WHO IS HE TO YOU?

"Valerie, don't you look radiant as always. You must be lost, because you don't visit us down here often," Nia said, as she giggled. "I love those earrings, Omar has good taste girl," she winked. Then she did a double take, "What's that big ass knot on your forehead?"

"Thanks, Nia. He sure does have good taste. Bird loves to spoil me from time to time," she responded ignoring her other question, just to make sure Tyra heard her only to look over and see she had disappeared from her desk. Val spotted her talking to another co-worker. She had a nice frame and face.

"I need to get back to work," Nia said and walked off.

Val heard Gail wrapping up her phone call but decided to head back to her office. She overheard someone say, "Someone knocked the shit out of her."

Val eased back in her office, just as her phone rang. She didn't recognize the number but answered it anyway.

"Val, long time no hear."

"Excuse me? Shai? Is that you?" she asked, recognizing her sister's voice, but not the number.

"Yes, this is my new number. I hope you are doing well, since we barely see you these days. Everything good?"

"Girl, you get a new number every six months," Val laughed. "And, yes everything is good. Just busy with work. What can I do for you?" Val asked, hoping her sister wouldn't ask her for any money.

"I was thinking, mommy's birthday is coming up. Let's give her a surprise birthday party. She hasn't had one in years and I think it's time."

"Sounds good to me. What are you thinking? I mean a theme, venue, food?"

"Well, The Georgia Aquarium did cross my mind and it's in my budget. The event area is nice. They also have a nice catering menu."

"Is this for you or mommy because she's not too fond of water over her head," Val responded laughing. Although she thinks the aquarium would be great. "What about Ventana's, downtown? She'll be in awe looking over the city and The Mercedes Benz Stadium."

WHO IS HE TO YOU?

"That's out of my budget. Ugh! You always do this, when I have an idea you always come up with something else, Val."

"Shai, chill! I only mentioned Ventana's because I have a connection over there and if it can save both of us money, then so be it. We can use it on the decorations, a DJ, or whatever."

"Fine! See if you can get it for October ninth and let me know."

"That's not that far out, a week before her birthday, but okay. Just have your money ready, I'm not footing the entire bill!"

"Bitch, bye!" Shai said and hung up.

Val knew Bret, the owner of Ventana's. He owns several locations and resided in Charlotte, North Carolina. He owed her a favor, so she planned on contacting him, as soon as she was done with Tyra, who was standing in her doorway when she looked up. Not sure what she wanted; Val was curious.

"Tyra, are you lost?" was the first thing that came out of Val's mouth.

"No, you have a moment?" she asked. Tyra didn't give Val time to respond; she closed the door and walked into her office, then politely took a seat.

"What can I do for you?"

"You can start by telling me the real reason you came downstairs. I sensed it wasn't to see Gail, but to see me. Yet I'm curious to know what you're fishing for."

Shocked, surprised, and stunned, Val stared at Tyra trying to read her. Tyra seemed worked up about something. She was a very pretty girl, with big eyes and red lipstick. She wore a bun on her head yet was professional looking.

"In a way, I did come to see you. I came across some information that really took me by surprise." Val held up the picture of her and Bird, so that Tyra could see it. "It was me, who helped you get this job, but I didn't know I was helping you to my fiancé either. He brought you to me as a friend, helping out a friend, but I never knew you were having relations with my man."

"Our man!" Tyra said in defense.

"Excuse me, because I don't see your name on any of our bills, mortgage, car notes or anything."

WHO IS HE TO YOU?

"That's because he's paying for those things at my residence. There's no need for my name to be on your residency," Tyra responded as if Val owed her something. She was very defensive. "I'm sorry if I sound harsh, but I'm tired of this charade as well. Bird and I have been together for three years now and he told me you were his roommate when he helped me get this job. The truth finally came out as I started working here. I'm not a home wrecker or whore by any means, because he has no problem showing me off."

"That's fucked up because as soon as you found out that we were together, you should have broken it off."

"Trust me, I tried several times, but it's not that easy when you love someone."

Val's head spun. Did she just say love? Val couldn't believe what she was hearing. Her fiancé's mistress sitting in her office saying she loves the man she sleeps with every night. How could that be? Bird was really doing a number on her.

"Yes, in the last three years, I've had two miscarriages and Bird is good with my son," she said. "Why haven't you broken it off, Val? You obviously know he's with me."

"Sweetheart, I just found this out this morning. Don't sit up here acting like you are a victim. Bird is with me every night, so when does he have time to be with you?"

"A man finds the time to be with who they want to be with," Tyra said as she stood. "Until you let him go, I guess he will continue to be our man!" she said as she opened the door and let herself out.

Emily quickly peeped inside, and then watched Tyra walk off. Val was angry. That bitch had the nerve to check her, for *her* man. Val couldn't believe that Tyra admitted to having an affair with Bird.

"What was that all about?" Emily asked.

Val couldn't hold her tears. She was scrambling trying to shut off her computer. Emily ran over to help Val, instead she ended up spilling coffee on her.

"Shit, Emily! Not you, too!"

"What, I'm sorry. What's going on?"

"I have to go; I have to get out of here now! If anyone needs me, I'll be working from home."

WHO IS HE TO YOU?

Val gathered her belongings and walked swiftly out the office. She dashed for her car, she heard her name being called, but kept walking, as she was clearly out of it. Once Val made it to her car, she quickly pulled out her inhaler. She hit her horn several times trying to calm herself down before driving. She didn't know what she intended to do once she faced Bird, but knew she had to.

CHAPTER FOUR

Val didn't know how she made it home safe, but she did. Through the tears and not being able to see while driving, she just knew she would hit something. When she arrived home, Bird wasn't there. Often, he worked remotely. Val took off her shoes and threw them across the room, she was not feeling well.

While she waited, she opened her laptop and then texted Bird. Val's heartbeat finally slowed down; earlier it felt like it was going to thump out of her chest. She heard her phone beep, knowing it was Bird, but then saw it was Shai.

"Going to call Bret now," was Val's response to Shai's text message.

Val located Bret's number in her phone and hit the send button. She was nervous simply because Bird could walk in at any given moment.

"Valerie Taylor, how may I help you?" Bret answered. "Sorry, let me start over. Valerie, how are you doing?"

Val chuckled because Bret always sounded so country, but intelligent as hell. His voice was one of a kind. "Bret, I'm good. Life has been treating me well. I hope the same for you."

"It has had its ups and downs this past year, but I'm surviving, I really can't complain," he said. "Girl it's been a minute. I hope your man is taking good care of you."

"Yes, of course. I wouldn't have it any other way," she chuckled watching the door. "I was hoping you can do me a favor," she said, jumping right to the point. "My sister and I plan to throw our mother a surprise birthday party and would like to book Ventana's. Not sure if you can accommodate us, but I'm hoping you can."

"How much you willing to spend?" he asked sounding nonchalant.

"What's the cost?" Val shot back, hoping for a discount. She usually supports her own, but since he owed her a favor, it was worth a try.

"I'm sure I can get you space on the date you would like, in exchange for a lunch outing to catch up. Also, it would be on the house, for you and for you only," Bret said and she could tell he was smiling on the other end of the phone, as he chuckled.

"Oh no, I have to give you something for the space as a fee and yes, to lunch and catching up," she agreed.

"You still have my email address?"

"Yes, I do. I will send you all the details as far as the date, time, how many expected, etc."

"Great! I'll get that taken care of for you. Also I'll be in town soon and I'd love to catch up."

"Sounds good," Val heard some keys at the door. "Bret, I have another call coming in. Please text me when you're in town," Val quickly said and ended the call, not sure if Bret had anything else he wanted to say. She struggled trying to clear out her phone as the door was opening.

"Sweetheart, I'm home and what are you doing here so early?" Bird asked.

"I felt lightheaded. I decided to bring my work home," Val said, wanting to jump all over Bird regarding Tyra, but needed to make sure he was settled first. She remained on the couch glancing at her computer screen, with a thousand questions.

WHO IS HE TO YOU?

Bird walked around like nothing was going on. "Sweetheart, did you eat anything or take something for your headache?" he asked concerned.

"Actually, I didn't feel lightheaded until I talked to Tyra Buffin, the girl I helped get a job," Val replied as Bird's demeanor changed.

"So, you talked to Tyra, about what? You got to make me understand why you became lightheaded after speaking with her."

Val moved her laptop to the table and then positioned her body to the edge of the couch, making sure she looked Bird in his eyes to see if he was lying.

"Rumor around the office is that you and Tyra have been having an affair long before I helped her get a job. Everyone knew except me. I felt like the biggest idiot on earth," Val said as she proceeded to stand, while getting agitated. "Bird, Tyra came into my office and confirmed what everyone has been saying, please, baby tell me it's not true?" Val asked hoping it wasn't true, but knew Tyra wasn't lying about sleeping with someone else's man.

Bird looked at Val in shock. He was obviously lost for words. He rubbed his beard instead as Val waited on a response. "Sweetheart, Tyra is old news. She's not important to me, you are."

Tears formed in Val's eyes. "So, you slept with her and then used me to help her ass get a job? All this time you guys were screwing each other? How dare you, Bird!" Val yelled in anger.

"Yes, we slept together, but what is it to you? It's old news. It was during a time when you left for three weeks to stay with your mom and I needed someone to talk to. Tyra just happened to be there. Val, I was vulnerable. You left me, and I didn't know if you were even coming back or not."

"Yet, during that time, I never slept with anyone! To make matters worse, you are still sleeping with that bitch, so what do you mean what is it to me? I can't believe you even put me in that position at work to be talked about, when you leave my office, then you head downstairs to her office. You know how embarrassing that is?" Val was so pissed, she picked up a candle holder wanting to throw it. Instead she wiped her tears, then placed the candle holder down and decided to leave the room.

Bird followed behind, Val. "Baby I'm sorry! I didn't mean to put you in that position." Just then, Bird's phone rang.

WHO IS HE TO YOU?

"Let me answer, to see if it's work."

Bird looked at his phone. Val quickly snatched it out his hands. "Hello."

"Valerie? What are you doing answering Omar's phone?"

"Who is this?"

"Tyra! Can you put Omar on the phone?"

Val hit the speaker button, as Bird fumes looking at Val in disgust. "Speak, he's listening."

"Omar, baby is everything okay? Did you finally tell Valerie about us?" Tyra asked.

"Tyra, right now is not the time," he answered in a calm tone.

"Well when is the right time? Don't forget about our event, this evening. Valerie is just going to have to understand," she said with no care in the world.

"Tyra don't you ever call this phone again! Whatever you had with Bird is over! You trifling bitch!" Val snapped.

"Val, give me the phone, please," Bird interjected as Tyra laughed in the background.

"Baby I'll talk to you soon. Please handle your side piece and let her know her position!" Tyra said and hung up.

Val shoved Bird his phone and shook her head in disgust. She couldn't believe Tyra had the audacity to call her the side piece. Bird didn't intervene as he should have.

"Don't you ever snatch my phone out my hand and answer it again! I'll handle Tyra! Do I make myself clear?" he ordered.

"You are pathetic! You and her can go to hell!"

Bird grabbed Val by her neck as his veins started to form in his arms. "Don't play with me, Val! I'll make sure Tyra knows her place, but I need you to get over it. Tyra is just a fuck thing, nothing more!"

"I can't breathe! Please, you are choking me!" Val said scratching Bird in the face to get him to let go, she then bit him on the hand.

WHO IS HE TO YOU?

"You bitch!" *WHAP!* His hand then went across Val's face. "Why are you keep putting me in the position to hit you? Can't you just play your part, Val?"

"You asshole! You cheat on me and then hit me for calling you out on your shit!" Val then started swinging on Bird. The sting to her face burned like hell.

Val and Bird were fighting like people on the streets. Bird dragged Val into the bedroom, where he kicked her in her side and hit her in her jaw. "You are going to learn not to cross me, again," he said as he continued to punch her.

The hit to the jaw knocked Val out. She laid on the floor thinking she was dying. She couldn't move, yet she felt like dying. Bird paced the room cursing while huffing and puffing. Val should have left well enough alone. She knew confronting Bird would probably end up with her getting hit, but she didn't care. She needed answers, yet it caused the one man she loved to death to treat her like a punching bag.

Val laid on the floor until she was out cold.

Val awakened to a bed full of roses. She was in so much pain. She looked around the room hearing humming and looked down to see she had on her nightgown.

She looked at the time, "Eight o'clock, I must have been out for some time," she whispered.

Bird walked into the room looking dapper in a tan suit. He was sharp. Val was confused to where he could be going.

"Sweetheart, I'm sorry about earlier. I don't need you worrying about Tyra. I need to be present at this event she's hosting that would be beneficial to my company," Bird said with no care in the world. "There is dinner in the microwave, again I'm sorry."

"Tyra, I remember now. You are going out with your mistress in public? How dare you, Bird!" Val yelled throwing a pillow at Bird, as she touched her throat remembering him choking her.

"Damn, I won't be out long! You should be grateful I'm coming back home to you!"

"After you fuck her?"

WHO IS HE TO YOU?

Bird walked closely over to Val, as she tried to position her body to the other side of the bed. She was terrified, as she didn't want any problem. "Sweetheart, I don't want to cause you any more pain than I have. I promise you, I won't be out long," he said picking up a box he had laid on the nightstand, that Val hadn't notice. "Open it."

Val opened the nicely wrapped box with tears in her eyes and noticed a Pandora heart engrave picture charm, with the word 'Forever.' She took it out and opened it. There was a tiny picture of them during their happier days inserted, which brought a smile to Val's face. She loved Bird with all of her. Yet, he couldn't see that. "Thank you."

"I love you, Valerie." He wiped the tears that streamed down her face. She knew in her heart that he loved her, but his demons got the best of him.

"Let me get to this event, so Tyra won't be calling me."

"Sure, go ahead. I'm sure she'll be calling anyway, but I know one thing. That bitch won't have a job for long!"

"Val, please don't do anything stupid you'll end up regretting," he replied, in Tyra's defense.

"Have a nice evening, Bird," Val said and threw the Pandora box at him. She climbed out of bed and pushed Bird out the room. The more she thought about him and Tyra the angrier she became. Luckily, Bird kept walking and exited the door. Val pulled herself to the couch and cried. She cried and cried, trying to think of ways to make him come back to her.

Val knew in her heart, that Bird really loved her, but didn't know how to love her the way she needed to be loved. She thought over the years, she could have changed him for the better. Some days were magnificent, and some were cloudy. She knew she had to convince Chanel to come back to the states and let Bird see Tyler. Not seeing his son was the only reason he acted out the way he did, but if Bird ever found out Val knew where Chanel was living, she'd be a dead woman.

Val had to get Chanel on the same page and just maybe, she'll see that Tyler needs both parents. Bird nearly killed Chanel, which was the reason for her disappearance, so she didn't know if that was possible.

CHAPTER FIVE

M eanwhile, Bird was having the time of his life with Tyra at her charity event for the homeless. Tyra is involved with three other friends of hers as they raised money for the homeless. They used the money to feed them throughout the years, as well as provide clothes, and update the shelters throughout Atlanta. This was Bird's first time being involved, and it was awesome to see so many people involved, as well as the Mayor of Atlanta, Keisha Lance Bottoms. He knew by joining Tyra it would increase his clientele. Although this was Tyra's purpose, she still worked until she was in a position to quit her day job.

Bird glanced at his buzzing phone and hit the ignore button to Val calling. She had sent several text messages, begging him to come home. She even insisted he bring Tyra back with him, if she meant that much to him. Bird laughed at the thought of them having a threesome. Although that didn't sound like a bad idea, Bird wanted to keep things the way they were.

Tyra walked up to Bird, with a wine glass in her hand. He knew once she started drinking, she got horney and that was a good thing. "Babe, I need you to smile at the camera," she said as the camera guy took a shot of them.

"Please let me know in advance when you decide to snap photos. I don't need Val getting in my shit about disrespecting her and her seeing it online somewhere, especially social media."

"You're already disrespecting her, by being here with me."

"She knows its business," he said, side eying Tyra.

"Is that so?" she responded, looking at him sideways.

Bird didn't respond. He was scoping out the scene, before he followed Tyra down the hall that lead to a dark, cold, storage room, in the back of the event hall. "Where the hell are we going?" he asked.

Tyra lead him to a room, where she locked the door, and then to a chair she had obviously placed there prior. She stood on her tiptoes and stuck her tongue inside of his mouth. Bird responded by deep throating her back, long and hard. He positioned his hands on her breasts and caressed them, until her nipples were hard. He then pulled up her dress, noticing she wasn't wearing any panties and smiled with excitement.

"What are you smiling about?" she whispered.

"What the hell do you think? That fat ass and that pussy wet, any man would smile to that shit. Just the way I like it."

"But it's just business, remember?" she said, responding to his comment earlier.

Tyra unbuckled his belt reaching in his briefs for his long hard dick as she started stroking it up and down. Tyra lead him to the chair, while his pants fell to the floor and positioned him to sit. She kneeled and then wrapped her soft lips around his big black dick. Bird moaned in excitement as he leaned his head back against the wooden chair. Tyra sucked his balls, and then moved her tongue to the tip of the head. She licked and slurped, just the way he liked it. She made sure she sucked it until his precum started to release on the tip of the head.

"Suck that dick, baby," he demanded. She took him all the way in, waiting on him to burst inside her mouth. "Baby, I need you to open wide. Daddy bout to make love to you in your mouth, just the way you like it."

Tyra usually got off by letting Bird cum in her mouth, this time she let up as she knew he was about to cum, pulled her dress over her hips and sat on his throbbing dick. "Tyra, baby what the fuck? Shit get up!" he ordered, but Tyra's pussy was so wet, she was riding him like that was the last dick left on earth. "You need to get up, I'm about to cum!"

She glided up and down his shaft, not listening to a word he said. Her frame was glued to his fat dick. She continued gyrating on him, as Bird gripped her ass and started hammering her as she sat on his shaft. He took her titties in his mouth one by one, and then stuck a finger in her anus, where she squirmed. Bird was starting to get a little too rough for Tyra. Her body shivered as she then climaxed. "Got damn!" she let out.

As soon as she released, he picked her up and pushed her against the wall with one leg slung over his shoulder. He started fucking Tyra as she became dry and it started to hurt. She was moaning out for Bird to stop; she didn't want to get too loud. "Babe, you're hurting me."

"That'll teach your ass not to disobey me again! When I tell you to get up, your ass get up! Now you want me to stop?" Bird asked as he continued to push his dick in and out of her.

"Baby, I'm sorry! Please stop, you are really hurting me!"

As Bird continued pumping in and out of her, she became agitated and bit him on the shoulder. "You, bitch!" *WHAP!* "What the hell you do that for?"

"You bastard!" she said holding her face as he released her. "Get the fuck out of here now!" she screamed, pushing him away from her, as she heard people starting to come near the door.

After Bird realized what he had done, he ran over to Tyra. "Sweetheart, I'm so sorry. I didn't mean to hit you! You bit me, and that shit hurt."

"Get your shit and get the hell out of here, before I scream again. Don't you ever put your hands on me! I don't know if that's some shit you do with Val, but not with me!"

Bird pulled up his pants and straightened his clothes, so he could sneak out the back entrance. He didn't want to continue with the event. If they were in private, he would have gotten Tyra all the way together.

She was going to learn to do what she was told. She knew better than to let him cum inside of her the way she did. She knew exactly what she was doing and didn't think consequences would follow.

CHAPTER SIX

The Following Day

Marc was furious that Val didn't have the report he emailed her prepared. He had threatened to let her go, if she didn't get it together. Val knew he was serious too. She had slipped one too many times in the last few weeks dealing with her personal life. Val had closed her door to concentrate, so she could have Marc's report ready by his meeting that afternoon. She couldn't understand how she let her personal life interfere with her work life; she knew how bad Marc had it out for her. Marc didn't believe Val earned her title and tried everything in his power to throw her under the bus.

It was hard for her to concentrate, given that Bird returned home after twelve a.m. smelling like ass, then had the nerve to ask her for sex. Val refused, then Bird got mad and slept on the couch. She was already upset with him for staying out as long as he did and then to return home, knowing he had sex with Tyra, was very disrespectful, but Val rolled with it. Val heard a knock on her door. Before she could say come in, Emily peeped her head in.

"Yes, what'cha need ma'am?" Val asked, not wanting to be interrupted.

"There is a Chanel on line two for you. She said she was family."

"Oh, yes. I'll take it. Sorry, I placed my calls on do not disturb, trying to finish this report. As a matter of fact. Why didn't you tell me Marc needed this right away?"

Emily looked confused and wondered why Val was asking her such a thing. "We spoke about this yesterday, before you ran out of here. I also sent out two emails from my phone, but you never replied back, Valerie," Emily said, trying to understand why it wasn't done. The report has been on Valerie's calendar for about a week.

"I didn't get to my emails. My apologies. I'll pick up the call."

Emily walked off, closing the door behind her.

"Hi Chanel. I was thinking about you and Tyler. I hope you both are doing well."

WHO IS HE TO YOU?

"Hi Valerie. We are. I got your text message late last night and couldn't make out what you were wanting from me."

Val had forgotten that she texted Chanel. She was all in her feelings and thought if Chanel eased her way back into Bird's life, it would make his life a lot easier. Chanel was a look-a-like for Chrissy Teigen at 5'2 and about one hundred and thirty-five pounds. Chanel had a round face and usually blonde hair, yet beautiful. Tyler was the spitting image of her and Bird. Val hasn't seen them both in years. She was just glad Chanel promised to keep in touch when she left for good.

"My apologies. I was having one of those days," Val kindly said. "I know this may sound blah, but Bird misses Tyler, so much. Personally, I know in my heart, he needs Tyler and wants to be a part of his life. He needs that," she pleaded.

"For one, you know that's not going to happen and secondly, Bird hasn't changed, I can tell that by the way you're talking. Bird tried to beat the baby out of me, remember?"

Val remembered it vividly, like it was yesterday. Bird was upset when he found out Chanel had cheated on him and was unsure that Tyler was his baby. When she came over to his apartment, he had beat her and tried to make her loose the baby at six months. Luckily the baby was born healthy. That was the first time Val had seen Bird so angry and put his hands on a woman, yet she stayed with him, through all his bullshit.

"I'm sorry. I was just hoping you'd find it in your heart to forgive him. Bird has really changed; I just know how much he misses his son."

"Does Bird know anything about us talking? I would hate for that to slip up."

"No, oh God no. He would...."

"Would what? Probably kill you and me!" Chanel said, knowing Bird hasn't changed and doesn't understand why Val is still with him. "Maybe in the near future, I'll bring Tyler around, but as a mother you have to respect my wishes."

"Chanel, I totally understand. Hopefully soon, everyone can be on the same page and move on. I just don't want Tyler to be grown and miss out on his father."

"Let me worry about that. Look I have to go. Discard my call and I'll talk to you later," she said and ended the call before Val could speak.

WHO IS HE TO YOU?

Val held the phone, hoping she could one day soon reunite Bird and Tyler, or would it be a mistake? She felt helpless and wanted so bad to give him a son, but that would be a disaster given the way he treats her. Finally, Val was able to put the phone away and proceed with work.

Two-hours later, Val's inability to perform at work was showing. She emailed Marc the wrong report and couldn't recall it. Moments later he was in her office giving her hell for sending him something that wasn't needed and on top of that late.

She resent the spreadsheet, but it was too late. He had asked Emily to send it to him earlier. Val was hurt, yet embarrassed. She wanted to scream, cry; but couldn't blame anyone but herself. Bird had her going crazy. She had to regroup before she was without a job.

Val heard a knock on her door and knew it was Emily because she texted her.

"Come in."

Emily walks in looking for answers. "What's going on, Val? Marc was really upset. I calmed him down and told him you were under a lot of stress and to please cut you some slack."

"Why you tell him that? I mean he don't need to know anything about me."

"Oh yes he does!" Emily said as she walked over to Val with her phone out. "This is the number one topic of the day." Emily positioned her phone so Val could see the Gala photo of Bird and Tyra.

Val put her hand over her mouth, not knowing about the very chummy photo of the two.

"Please explain this, as Tyra is freely downstairs discussing her very epic evening of her event. People are speculating if you two are together, but by the look on your face and neck, I can tell you two had a disagreement."

Emily saw right through Val and knew every time Bird put his hands on her, her demeanor changed and the bruises end up showing through the makeup she added on her body.

"Bird thought it was a good idea to go to the event for his marketing business. I didn't know about the photo."

"So you ran out of here yesterday to talk to Bird, I'm sure. Did he admit anything with Tyra?"

WHO IS HE TO YOU?

Val felt her body shutting down, not wanting Emily to judge her nor did she want to answer her question. "Yes, he did admit to being with her once."

"That's bullshit and you know it, Val! That explains the bruises you are carrying. Did he hit you because you asked him about it? What is it, Val...Oh I got time today!" Emily said getting worked up.

"Why does it matter to you? I mean you aren't dealing with this, I am!" Val responded getting defensive.

"Because I've been in your shoes and you know it! I know the signs because I've worn the same bruises you're carrying. All you're doing is making excuses for him!" Emily started pacing back and forth. "And on top of that, home girl is having a field day with it!"

"Emily, I'm sorry. I know your history; it's just I know Bird needs help and I can help him. If only I can help him get his son back, he'll be fine."

Emily leaned in close to Val. "Just listen to yourself. His son can't help him, and surely you can't. Get out now, while you're still alive! Your career is hanging by a thread!"

Just then there was a knock on her door. "Come in."

Both ladies looked up. "Surprise," Bird said walking in with a dozen roses. The receptionist walked away, as Emily started walking towards the door as well to exit. She gave him an evil look and walked out of Val's office. She wanted to punch him so bad.

"What a surprise," Val said, extending her hands out to receive the roses. "They are lovely."

"Just like my lovely woman," he said standing looking at Val. "Yo, why your girl gave me the evil stare?"

"I guess you're talking about Emily? If so, I had no clue she gave you an evil stare."

"Usually she speaks, but this time she gave me the stank look."

"Not to change the subject, but you could have warned me about the photo of you and Tyra. It could have saved me the embarrassment."

"Shoot, I'm sorry. I forgot all about that. It was an innocent photo," he said, cutting his eyes at Val. "I wanted to stop by because I missed you. Maybe we can go out to dinner later, if you got time for a brother, and then maybe when we get home I can make love to my beautiful woman."

Val was just wondering what Bird was up too or wanted. In her heart, she knew he had slept with Tyra the night before but wanted her to forgive him of his wrongdoing. She wanted that moment they were having to last forever.

"When you get home this evening, it's all about you. I've already laid out your attire. All you have to do is show up," he said closing in on Val, giving her the smoothest kiss ever. At that moment, Val felt like she was in love, just for a moment. She enjoyed the good times with him and would do anything to keep it that way. As Bird was about to leave, Val decided to walk him out. There was no way he was leaving her office, going to see Tyra. She made sure everyone saw them as they exited her office. If they were going to talk about something, might as well give them something to talk about.

CHAPTER SEVEN

Later That Evening...

Val was sitting at a table alone, waiting on Bird to arrive. After she arrived home from work she was ordered to get dressed for a night to remember. Bird had left her a few texts to follow, as he hired someone to do her hair and makeup. The dress Bird laid out for Val to wear was a midi emerald green dress with sequins and lace, matched with a pair of gold pumps with emerald green stones, as well as matching accessories.

She felt and looked like a real princess. She took snap shots of herself and posted on her Snapchat and Instagram page. She hadn't felt pretty in a long time and it made her feel extra sexy. The dress looked like it was painted on, it was a perfect fit. Val didn't know what Bird had in store for their night, but after the night and day she had, she planned to enjoy every moment.

WHO IS HE TO YOU?

She strolled on her social media page as she waited and came across the photo of Bird and Tyra from the Gala, she then decided to stalk Tyra's page. It wasn't private, so she strolled freely. Her stomach started turning in knots when she came across a video of her at work thanking the love of her life for the roses she received and tagged the person. Val noticed the video was from two weeks ago and clicked on the person tagged. The person seemed anonymous, but Val knew that tattoo a mile away. The person had an anonymous name and the photo was of a man with his back turned, hat low, but revealed the tattoo of a little boy on his arm. It was clearly Bird. Val didn't know anything about his Instagram page. They both share a Facebook page, but barely post because of their business. Val was crushed, but how would she bring it up during a night of pure bliss, she wondered.

Val dropped her phone, as she felt a tap on her back and jumped.

"Sweetheart, oh my. What a surprise," Val responded turning around to Bird handing her more beautiful roses. She kissed him, then took the roses and placed them on the table as she reached for her phone.

"Stand. I want to see your beautiful frame, in that sexy ass dress."

She did as she was told, as people watched on and turned around a few times, smiling like a schoolgirl.

"Damn, you look great! I'm so glad you could join me. I wanted you to feel like the queen you are and honor you," he said looking in Val's eyes.

"Awe, thank you, baby. You have really made my night. From the dress, hair, and makeup, you've outdone yourself."

Val wanted so bad to ask what the occasion was but took her seat instead. Bird had her special wine sent to the table, Prosecco, a sparkling wine from Italy, she enjoyed drinking. She wasn't going to ruin the moment by bringing up another chick that didn't matter, but knew Tyra was somewhere in the background waiting on her to slip up.

Bird looked so yummy in his fitted suit. He had a fresh clean cut and a shave, and the smell of his Burberry cologne was to die for. Her man was an eyeful. Val couldn't stop blushing; she was feeling good for once.

"So, baby what's good? You haven't done this in a while," Val softly spoke.

WHO IS HE TO YOU?

"You, Val, it's all about you tonight. I told you earlier I wanted to make your night special. I know things have been crazy with us, but I appreciate you. I'm just trying to be the man you need."

"This means a lot to me. I needed this. For a moment, I thought you had forgotten about me," Val said winking at Bird. She then took on a more serious tone, "I love you so much, Omar, despite the bullshit you put me through, but I know we are destined to be together."

"I want to make you the happiest woman on this earth."

Val wasn't prepared when Bird got down on one knee. The waiter came by and filled the wine glasses, as Val put her hand over her mouth. "Valerie Renee Taylor, I love you so much. I would not be complete if it wasn't for you. I am asking you to do me the honors of being my wife, the incomparable Mrs. Mize," he said taking Val by the hand, as he pulled out a 2.25 carat, round, diamond ring. It was the same ritani masterwork cushion halo band, Val and Bird looked at months ago. She couldn't believe after all these years; Bird was finally asking her to marry him.

"Yes, baby, yes! I'll marry you!" Val said in excitement and tears as patrons in the restaurant looked on and clapped. She was overjoyed and head over heels. She looked at the rock on her finger and then gave Bird the biggest kiss, ever. "I love you, Omar Mize."

"Love you more, baby!"

They both calmed down so that they could order their food. Val kept looking at her finger in disbelief. She knew he would one day propose to her, but after years of waiting, she kindly gave up waiting. She didn't know what her mother would say after telling her the good news, she just hoped she would be happy for them.

Val waited patiently at the restaurant. She summoned her mom and sister to lunch at the Vortex, as Shai suggested. Of all the restaurants in Atlanta, she wanted a burger. She was still in disbelief with Bird, as they made sweet love all night long. Val prayed for those moments. Bird got up and cooked breakfast, giving Val permission to go pamper herself.

She did just that. She started out at the spa, then headed out to get a mani and pedi, and then she was able to get her hair washed and trim. She felt good and looked good. As she waited she dialed Bird to see if she needed to bring him something to eat for later, but his phone went to voicemail. She dialed it again and heard static.

"Hello, Sweetheart."

There was laughter in the background, and she could have sworn she heard a female giggle. Val looked at her phone and then got a click, as the phone hung up.

"Babygirl, you look so beautiful," Val's mom, Thelma said approaching the table. Val placed her phone on the table and stood to greet her mother.

"Hey, Shai."

"What's up big sister."

They all took a seat, as the waiter came and took everyone's drink order. Val's spirit was dampened, trying to figure out where Bird was and with whom. Just then, her phone rung and it was him.

"Sweetheart, where are you?" Val asked, quickly picking up her phone.

"Hey, I came to the store to pick up a few items. Need anything?"

"No, I was calling to ask you the same thing."

"No, babe, I'm good. Have fun and don't worry about me. I'll see you at home."

Before she could say I love you, he hung up. Val's mind was now all over the place.

"Babygirl, what is that rock on your finger?" Thelma asked, raising a brow.

"Oh, this thing," Val responded pointing to the ring on her finger. "It's just an engagement ring! Bird and I are finally engaged," she said in pure joy. Shoving her ring in Thelma and Shai's face.

Shai kept playing with her cell phone, giving her sister a fake smile. Neither of the ladies showed any enthusiasm. They both looked at each other.

"So I get it. That's why we're here? So you can break the news about your engagement to us?" Shai hinted.

"Well damn, you could have showed me some love. We're getting married, not dying!"

WHO IS HE TO YOU?

"And if you stay in that relationship, that's where it may head," Shai replied.

"Babygirl. The ring is nice and all. I just wish I could be happy for you. Maybe with someone else, who doesn't hit you," Thelma interjected, waving down the waiter.

"Mom, it was once and Bird got some help. He was under a lot of stress. We are good now," Val claimed.

"That's what you call a few months ago, when you called me to get a break from him? Valerie Renee Taylor, I know a cover up when I see it and you are in total denial. Now I raised you better than this. Bird is going to break you! Literally!" Thelma pleaded.

Shai wanted to speak, but instead shook her head. She loved her sister deeply but couldn't see why she couldn't see Bird for what he was.

"Sweetheart, I love you and only want to see you happy. If you marry him, I think you'll be more miserable," Thelma continued.

"Mom, I'm not miserable. Stop acting like all Bird does is beat me. He hit me one time!" Val said in defense.

"Is that so?" Shai finally spoke. "Look I don't care what you do, just make sure you're doing it for the right reasons."

Val was getting irritated at Shai for her remark, which means she's been talking to Thelma. Val had confided in Shai about an incident months ago, which caused Bird to lay hands on her. All she wanted was them to be happy for her.

Val took a deep breath and smiled. "Thanks mom and Shai, but I'm happy. Let's just order our food and talk about the engagement later."

"And nothing on my end will change how I feel, Val. It's your decision, not mine!" Thelma said.

As they ordered and prepared for their food, they managed to talk about other things besides Bird. Thelma brought up the upcoming presidential election, all were hoping for a win with Joe Biden. Val was glad to hear Shai received a promotion on her job and hoped that put an end on her asking Val for money until payday.

WHO IS HE TO YOU?

Once the food arrived, everyone became silent. Val glanced over at her mom, who was heavily into her food. Val ordered the Yankee Rueben sandwich, with onion rings. She preferred to have seafood, but the sandwich wasn't bad at all. Shai tried to talk but had a mouth full of food. Val and Shai's relationship was starting to bloom because in the past they could not get along. Shai thought Val was bougie and bragged about how much money she made, while Val was envious of Shai's long hair and *I don't give a fuck* attitude. Once they sought therapy from their Pastor, they promised to work on their relationship.

"I hope I'm the maid of honor," Shai said laughing.

"Well you can be, but I want to elope."

"What!" Thelma said almost choking. "See, something is wrong with this picture. Did it cross your mind on why he asked you to marry him?"

"Because he loves me, that's why! Damn, ma if I want to elope, that's my decision. I wanted to tell you guys my happy news, but it seems to have backfired!" Val responded in anger. She was tired of her mom's remarks. Just then, Val's phone rang.

"Babe, I miss you," Bird said on the other end.

"Miss you, too."

"Just calling to check on you. I know your family is probably talking bad about me, but I will prove them wrong," Bird responded, putting a smile on Val's face. "Now hurry up and get home. I'm ready to go half on a baby."

Val couldn't believe what she was hearing. She didn't think Bird wanted kids because he never talked about it. Val got anxious, "I'll be there soon, babe."

"I see that glow on your face. He must have had something good to say," Shai said.

"Yes. I'm going to leave money for the food and head out. I got a very important appointment," Val replied smiling.

Val kissed her mom and sister goodbye and reached for her shades. All she thought about was one day, giving Bird a son. It wouldn't replace Tyler, but she knew that he would be happy and content. Val wanted to stop by Starship before heading home, to pick up a few items to spice things up in their bedroom.

If she knew one thing, she knew how to please Bird. Him going outside their relationship had nothing to do with her. She knew her and Bird had to be on the same page, if he wanted them to work.

CHAPTER EIGHT

The vibrator penis ring didn't sit well with Bird, but it did wonders for Val. The vibration along with penetration gave her multiple orgasms. She didn't understand why Bird didn't enjoy it, but she couldn't tell, the way he was deep inside her.

"Babe what do you think of inviting someone to our bedroom?" Bird asked while he was inside of Val.

"What do you mean; a threesome?" Val responded through moans.

"Someone to spice things up. I think you would enjoy it as well."

Val clawed her nails into Bird's back, as her body and legs trembled with another orgasm. She was sweating, trying to catch her breath, while Bird laid inside her trying his hardest to cum.

WHO IS HE TO YOU?

"What's the problem babe?" she asked, trying to figure out why he was having trouble climaxing.

"I'm going limp. I'm trying to bust a nut, but you just lying there."

Val had put in all the work. Bird only came once, now he wanted her to do more work. He gave up, pulled out, and turned over on his back.

"What do you think about Tyra?" he asked. "She would consider the invitation, if the opportunity presented itself."

"Are you suggesting a threesome with your fucking mistress?" Val responded. "Oh I see where this is going. You get the best of both worlds in one setting," Val said angrily, sitting up facing Bird.

"Technically, yes I will, but you'll also get an experience of a lifetime," he said.

"The bitch must turn flips or something during sex," Val shot back. "Talking about an experience of a lifetime!"

Bird laughed, like that was the funniest thing ever. He couldn't hold it in. Val's facial expression was sickening. He stopped laughing because he needed Val to see why bringing in a third party would be good for them. "Babe, it doesn't have to be Tyra at all. You can find the right person. I only mentioned Tyra because that was the first person that came to mind."

Val couldn't believe Bird was offering Tyra out of all people. She looked at her fiancé and knew he was still sleeping with her. Not only that, he had feelings for her too. She didn't know what to think, given he had proposed to her. Val knew if she agreed to Tyra joining them, then just maybe after it's all said and done, he can get Tyra out of his system and they can move on.

"I'll think about it. Maybe I need to see what kind of hold she has on you."

Bird beamed just a little. He knew he was close to having what he wanted. The thought of fucking two females at once was every man's dream. Bird now had to get Tyra to agree to having a threesome and he knew that wasn't an easy task.

He looked over at Val, who had her lips poked out. He knew he caught her by surprise by mentioning Tyra, but any woman would do. Val was good at what she did, but Bird wanted more excitement and he knew Tyra was the perfect fit and since Val loved him so much, she'd do anything he asked.

WHO IS HE TO YOU?

Val started to go shower before Bird summoned her back. "Where you going?"

"To shower. You want to join me?"

"I will after you give me some head. I mean I haven't come. You got off and you're good to go," Bird pointed out, making Val feel bad.

"Sweetheart, I've already went down on you. I'm tired."

"A wife doesn't get tired of pleasing her man. You know the saying. What one woman won't do, another one will," he said, looking over at Val until she found her way to his dick.

Val felt pressured and knew if she didn't, he would be over Tyra's place in a heartbeat. She wanted her man to love her and only her and just didn't understand what was going on with Bird, but she put her warm mouth on his dick and sucked away.

Bird felt Val's pain and continued to push his manhood in and out her mouth. He was moaning as he felt her teeth clamp strapping the walls of his manhood. Val took all of him in and was about to let go, until Bird forced her to stay put, releasing his seeds in her mouth.

"Babe, swallow that shit!"

Val spit his seeds out on the carpet before she knew it. She couldn't swallow. She felt Bird's eyes on her and then felt uneasy about what she had done.

"Tyra takes that shit like a pro!" Bird bragged, not realizing what he had just said, as he eyed his fiancé.

"You motherfucker! How dare you tell me what the fuck your whore does and then you want me to invite her in our bedroom? Bullshit!" Val yelled, and threw a pillow in Bird's direction. "Let her suck you dry from now on!" She added, as she stumbled across the room.

"Val, I didn't mean anything by it," Bird stated, trying to clean up his mess he just made with his comment. He jumped from the bed and ran into the bathroom behind her. "Babe, I'm really sorry."

Val pushed him away. He wrapped his arms around her, trying to make her understand, but she kept resisting. "Bird, please, let me go. I can't do this right now!" she demanded.

"Do what?" he asked, pushing her away from his grip. "Val, you always fucking up the mood. Why can't you just go with the flow? I asked you to swallow, instead you spit. What kind of shit is that?"

WHO IS HE TO YOU?

"What kind of shit is it when you ask me to marry you, but bring up your mistress every chance you get? If she can do it better, why didn't you ask her to marry you?"

"Because I asked you, bitch!" Bird said, and then went to slap Val. "Don't ask me any more questions. You hear me?"

"Yes!" Val hollered, holding her face in distress.

"You better not start that crying, I didn't even hit you hard enough. Now get your ass in the shower and you going to suck my dick when you get out!"

Val had a burning sensation to her face. She tried to hold back the tears, wondering what she had done wrong. Bird treated her like shit as if she did something wrong. Val turned the shower on as Bird pushed her inside. He got in and closed the shower door. Val adjusted the water temperature to his liking. Val got down on her knees as the water ran through her hair and took him in her mouth. Val did her usual, sucked his balls, played with the tip of his head, but wasn't into it and could tell Bird was getting agitated.

"Babe, get up and bend over. I ain't got time to be playing with your ass. You don't want to swallow, that's cool. I'll just ram my dick in your ass, then!"

As soon as Val could get in position. Bird ran in her so rough, he was tearing up her insides. She wanted to scream but put her hand over her mouth through the pain. He pumped in her so hard, her head started hurting. Tears started to fall and Val was really in pain. Her heart rate was over the normal and she couldn't do anything but take it.

"Bird you're hurting me, please stop."

He continued as he grabbed her by her waist, slowing up his rhythm, pushing in and out and watching his dick take a glide inside her walls. Then he rammed back in Val. She couldn't take it anymore. She pushed him out of her.

P-O-P! "Don't ever do that shit again!" He then took another jab at Val, hitting her in her shoulder and stomach. "You're going to have to do a better job at pleasing me!"

Bird exited the shower, while Val balled up in a fetal position in the corner of the shower crying her eyes out, as the water started to get cold. She was in so much pain, that the water temperature didn't matter. She didn't think she could go through with a wedding if it wasn't going to get any better. Val was growing more and more terrified of Bird and his demands.

CHAPTER NINE

Val was meeting up with Shai and the party planner to go over everything for Thelma's surprise birthday party at Ventana's, but when she arrived she didn't see anyone's car parked outside. She started to dial Shai's number until someone peeped outside a side door and waved at her.

She noticed it was Marianne, the party planner, then got out her car and made her way inside.

"Hello, Valerie. It's nice to finally meet you," she said extending her hand out.

"Good to meet you as well," Val said, noticing Shai on her phone. "Where did you guys park? I didn't see any cars."

"We parked on the other side. You came in through the back entrance. We saw you in the back; that's how we knew you were out there."

WHO IS HE TO YOU?

"Val, girl you are going to love the lay out Marianne has for mommy's party. It's going to be awesome!" Shai said, ending her phone call. "So glad we can do something nice for her," Shai added nudging Val in the side.

"Damn it, Shai, that hurts!"

"My bad. I barely touched you. Are you okay?"

"Yes, it just hurts."

Marianne pulled out her layouts and color schemes for the party. She led them to the room where the party would be held and images of the party decor. Val was really impressed with Bret's venue; it was more than she expected.

"I like the pink and gold decor," Val said.

"I do to, but I think Shai likes black and silver."

"Because Black is mommy's favorite color. We never see her in other colors," Shai added.

"We need to change that. Your mom is royalty, a queen. These colors would do her justice, you'll see," Marianne added.

"I trust your judgment. Let's go with pink and gold," Val chimed in.

Shai rolled her eyes. She was not feeling the colors but looked over at Val who was holding her side, like Shai kicked her in it. She didn't know what was up with Val, but something was off.

"You will take care of the food, silverware..." Shai said not finishing her sentence.

"We will take care of everything. All you have to do is pay the bill," Marianne replied.

"Great! You can send the bill to my sister," Shai said laughing.

Val made a smirk, not really into what was going on. Shai approached her squeezing her tight. "Sister, what's going on? You okay?"

"Ouch, I'm fine. You keep touching me and it hurts!"

Shai pulled back as Marianne looked on trying to figure out what was going on. Before Val knew it, Shai pulled up her blouse and noticed a nasty bruise.

WHO IS HE TO YOU?

"I see why you are hurting. That's a nasty bruise you got there," Marianne pointed out.

Shai put her hand over her mouth looking at Val in disbelief. Val quickly pulled her blouse down, embarrassed.

"Are we done here?" Val asked.

"Yes, I think so. If anything else, I'll be in touch," Marianne replied, confused to what was going on.

Val grabbed her belongings to head out the door.

"Val you just wait right there," Shai demanded. "Marianne, thank you. Talk soon," she added, as Marianne hurried and got out the room. Nothing made sense to her.

Val turned around to Shai, pissed. "Don't you ever do that again!"

"It's sad that the ones that care the most are the ones that get pushed to the side. You were in a funk since you got here and especially after I nudged you in your side. I watched you in pain. That bruise isn't pretty. So are you going to tell me you fell on Bird's fist?"

"You bitch! You always thinking Bird is hitting on me. Why won't you go find a man who may be into marrying you? Is that what this is all about?"

Shai wanted to slap the daylight out of Val, but that would be too easy, given she's already carrying enough bruises. "I'll take being a bitch any day, over someone's personal punching bag! I can't believe I've envied you all these years, only to find out, you're the weak one! Letting that man with no value beat the shit out of you!"

"Shai, you've always been jealous of me!"

"I used to be. Given what I know, you ain't got shit I want!" Shai said wiping tears from her eyes. "Val, I love you and you don't even see that. This moment is supposed to be something special for mommy. I bet under those clothes, you got a million bruises and you going to marry that turd," Shai added, as she tried to caress Val's face. She was concerned about her sister.

"Please don't touch me and I mean it!"

Shai took two steps back. "I'll be praying for you. Also, find some other makeup that will do justice for that bruise on your face."

Shai picked up her belongings and exited the door. Shai was so hurt, that she had every intention to put a cap in Bird's ass. She wanted to hire some goons that would take him out, but was it worth it?

Val stayed behind as she took out her compact mirror and packed more makeup on her face. Her body was in so much pain. Her shoulder and stomach ached. She couldn't wait to soak in some warm water and Epsom salt.

She wished it was that easy to just leave, but it wasn't. The thought of starting over and dating, didn't sit well with her. Bird wasn't a bad person; he just didn't know how to control himself. He was really caring.

After a full day, Val hurried home to cook dinner. She wanted it to be an easy night since she had work to do on the computer. She prepped her onions, green peppers, and mushrooms as she wanted to make a dish of baked spaghetti, garlic bread, and a fresh salad.

Val set the table and placed two wine glasses on it. She also thought about having a dinner for Bird's mom and siblings since she hasn't seen them in forever and wondered if Bird told his mom about the engagement. After Val left the venue earlier, she stopped and looked at a few wedding dresses. She was so excited that she couldn't wait to start planning after her mom's birthday party.

She was still a little sore in the shoulders, so she popped two ibuprofen. Bird hadn't made it in, so Val hoped to have dinner ready for him. He rarely likes to eat out but expected her to have a decent meal waiting on him. As she started to prepare a fresh garden salad, her phone rang.

Val let it ring a few times before picking it up.

"Hello, mother. How are you?" she said answering.

Hey, sweetheart. I just got done eating dinner and had you on my mind. What are you up to?"

"I hope that's a good thing. I'm cooking one of your favorite dishes, baked spaghetti," Val said, sipping on a glass of wine.

"I'm calling because I spoke to your sister earlier and she told me something very disturbing. Is Bird still beating on you?"

Val was not in the mood to be interrogated. She couldn't believe Shai went running her mouth. She didn't get in her business, so why was she in hers? Val rolled her eyes, not wanting to answer her mother.

"I take that as a yes, since it's taking you too long to answer. Val, I hope you know marrying him is only going to make the beatings worse. I don't want to lose my daughter due to domestic violence, so I'm pleading with you to get out!" Thelma said, hoping her daughter was listening.

Val hit the speaker button on her phone, so that she could put on a mitten to put the spaghetti in the oven. "Mom, everything is okay. Shai is always jumping to conclusions and you know that. Bird isn't as bad as you guys think he is."

"That punk better fall back, because I know a woman beater when I see one. I will put a cap in his ass if he continues to hit you and you....I can't believe you allow him to hit you, Val. I'm totally shocked!"

"Mom, please. It's not what you think."

"If that's the case, I'll be over there shortly so I can examine your body and if there are any bruises, I will deal with Bird personally, before getting someone to lay him..."

Before Thelma could finish, Bird pressed the end button on Val's phone and ended the call. Val jumped and also burned herself. She did not hear Bird come in and was terrified of how much he had heard. Bird opened the fridge and grabbed a bottle of water, waiting for Val to open her mouth; instead she just stood, not wanting to move.

"What the hell is your mother talking about? That old bitch, got a lot of nerve talking about putting a cap in my ass," Bird said laughing. He hit the countertop with tears in his eyes. "Val, your mama really think she can do me?"

"Bird, please, nothing is funny," Val managed to say.

"She better not come over here, if she knows what's good for her. Why the fuck she's in our business anyway? I ought to hit your ass for entertaining that bullshit on the phone, you should have hung up!"

"Bird, that is my mother and she's concerned!"

"I don't give a fuck if that's Michelle Obama, she ain't got no business being in our business," Bird said walking towards Val as she jumped, instead he kissed her on the cheek. "Set the table, I'll be ready to eat shortly."

WHO IS HE TO YOU?

Val knew her blood pressure was up. Her heartbeat started racing. All she wanted was to be happy and she wasn't. She didn't want Bird to do anything crazy, especially to her mother or sister. Val didn't know how to take Bird because he alienated himself from his family and only talk to his mom every now and then. Val tried to force Bird to have a relationship with his mother, but it always cause friction between them, so she left it alone. She knew inviting his mother and siblings to dinner was just a thought.

Val took the spaghetti out the oven and prepared Bird a salad. Val wasn't all that hungry, but knew she had to sit at the table with Bird, or he'd think something was wrong. When Bird came back into the kitchen, Val had his dinner ready and pulled out his chair for him.

"Babe, did you stop taking your birth control pills yet?"

"Well, no."

"How do you expect to get pregnant, if you don't?"

Val really wanted to give Bird a son but was scared. She thought long and hard because of what he subjected her to and didn't know if bringing a child into the relationship was very wise, especially after what

Chanel went through. Val knew she should have said yes to Bird but knew if she did, he would asked to see them.

"I need you to bring the rest of them to me, so I can assure you won't be taking them. It's time we start our own little family, starting tonight," he said. "I knew you were still taking the pills weeks ago, after you rushed home from being with your mom and sister. I saw the pills in your purse."

"Why tonight?" Val asked raising a brow.

"I have a surprise for you. So after dinner, I need you to go freshen up and put on your best lingerie," Bird smirked. "Tyra will be joining us."

"Bird, please. I thought I would decide who. I work with Tyra and don't think that's very wise of her to be joining us. Besides, I don't think I'm ready."

Bird continued to eat, while he side-eyed Val. She knew if she didn't do as he said, she would pay for it later. She had never had a threesome, never been with a female and was scared out of her mind. Better yet, her man's side chick. Val's feelings were more than crushed that he had invited Tyra behind her back.

CHAPTER TEN

Bird waited patiently on Tyra to join him for lunch. He ordered their usual. He wanted to know what was really so important that she couldn't show up to meet him and Val the night before. Although Val was relieved, Bird was disappointed.

The waiter arrived with their food just as Tyra walked in. Bird got up to greet her and pulled her chair out to sit.

"Sorry I'm running behind. Traffic was awful," she stated.

"No worries. As you can see I went ahead and ordered, so you wouldn't have to rush back to work. How are you?" Bird asked, trying to see where Tyra's head was at.

"I appreciate it. I'm good, thanks for asking."

"Let's just cut to the chase, what happened to you? I mean we had a deal and you gave me this sorry excuse about why you couldn't make it," Bird remarked.

"I ran into your fiancé, who flaunted her ring around, as if you aren't still sleeping with me, a reason for the no show. I thought long and hard about it and decided it was best. I don't want to sleep with Val! You just gave me money to have an abortion, telling me it wasn't a good time to have a baby, then propose to that bitch, but still at my house playing house. What's your deal, Bird or should I say Omar?" Tyra exclaimed.

Bird was loss for words. He forgot all about Tyra having an abortion and then he proposed to Val, not thinking she would find out. Val is not the one to go around the office opening her mouth, but I guess she felt compelled to. He tried to find the right words to make it right with Tyra, before she snapped.

"I'm totally sorry, my apologies. I never meant to hurt you with the abortion or the proposal. Val pressured me and if she left, then I wouldn't be able to help you financially," he declared, as Tyra rolled her eyes.

Bird often lied to Val about the money he used out of their account to help Tyra. That was his way of keeping her around. He laid his hands on top of hers, with a deep sincere look. She wasn't buying his lies, and knew what he was about, but he was good with helping her with her son.

"Also, don't ever put your hands on me ever again. That stunt you pulled at the Gala was a major turn off. Bird you hit me and thought it was okay. I'm not a punching bag, like Val."

"I told you I didn't mean it. I don't know what came over me, sweetheart, I'm sorry."

"What about Val? I mean, I can see her bruises and clearly everyone else does."

Bird was getting worked up. Tyra was sticking her nose in something that didn't concern her. Val was his main woman and what he did with her was nobody's business. If Tyra conducted herself accordingly, maybe she would be in Val's position, with a ring. That's why she was his side bitch.

"Val is not being abused in any way. I don't know what you or anyone else is seeing; maybe I need to examine her body myself. This is news to me," he assured.

Tyra ate the rest of her food and so did Bird. There was a slight silence, before Tyra handed Bird a copy of her son Kiyan's basketball schedule. "He would be glad to see you there, if you can make it."

"Thank you! I would be glad to show up and surprise him. He reminds me of…"

"Who? He reminds you of whom, Bird?"

"My nephew, back in Philly. I don't get to see him often, but he sends me video clips," he answered lying. Kiyan reminded him of his own son, Tyler. "Kiyan is something special."

"Thank you for being there for him. You are really good with him, that's why it was so hard for me to go through with the abortion after so many miscarriages."

Bird wanted her to stop with all the abortion talk. He got it, but he couldn't have a baby by her, knowing Val's situation. He was glad she went through with it though. The waiter came over and offered refills, before dropping off the check. Bird picked it up and paid the waiter the bill.

"So where do we go from here?"

"I'm not sleeping with your fiancé, that's for sure. You got to really drop some large bills for that to happen," Tyra said jokingly to Bird, who laughed at her comment. "Besides, you need to figure out who you want to be with. She has a ring on her finger; I don't."

"A ring doesn't mean a thing."

"Don't I know!" she shot back. "Look I gotta get back to work."

"I'll be in touch. I'll see you tonight," he said smiling. They both stood up to leave. He kissed her on her cheek, "Love you, Tyra."

She shook her head and walked off. That was one time Bird didn't get what he wanted and that was for Tyra to agree to the threesome again. If she thought she was the only one, she could think again, but it would happen. Bird always thought that Val could make him completely happy and he kept convincing himself, but he still found himself seeking love elsewhere. He didn't know what it was.

Bird decided to call and have flowers delivered to Val, just because she puts up with his bullshit. The little things kept her happy. He also decided to throw in a box of candy from the flower shop with his order. After that, Bird thought it was time to sit down with a private investigator or somebody that could help track Chanel down with his son. He knew if he caught up with her alone, he would kill her for lost time.

His anger with her runs deeper than anyone would imagine. He thought they would be a family, until the unthinkable happened and she took his son away. Not one person knew where she was. Bird had her family investigated, phones tapped and nothing came up. After a lot of money spent, he let it go, but knew it was time. He just hopes his son would remember him before it was too late.

CHAPTER ELEVEN

Birthday Surprise...

The day had come and Val was overly excited because everything was so beautiful. Although this was Shai's idea, Val still forked out more than half the money as usual, but what did she expect fooling with her sister? Other than that, Val was just excited for her and Bird to get some time together. She booked the Marriott for their stay, so they wouldn't have to drive back home. She even packed some sexy lingerie for the evening.

The venue was decorated nicely, in the pink and gold colors. A picture booth, nice floral arrangements, pink and gold rose petals everywhere, a balloon garland, a sweets table, and a big beautiful three-layer Chanel cake, for the queen. The staff had everything set for the evening. Val was dressed in a fitted jumpsuit that filled every curve she had. Bird wasn't pleased with her attire, but she refused to give in and change her clothes. Bird only felt comfortable with Val wearing skimpy outfits if it's just him and her and if he picked it out. Val thought it was cute in the beginning, and then realized it was a control thing.

"Babe, which bow tie you suggest?" Bird asked Val, holding up two ties near his neck.

"The one on your right. It complements the slacks you have on."

Bird moped around the room taking his time, as if they didn't need to get to the venue. "So how long are we planning on staying? I'm not too fond of your family you know."

"Sweetheart until it's over, or you can come back to the room if you like. It's my mom's birthday party," Val said, trying not to argue.

"If I leave, you leave. Got that?" he demanded.

"But, I..."

"What, can't leave?"

Val stood impatiently waiting on Bird. He gave her a stern look, waiting on her to answer him.

"Sure," was all she said.

WHO IS HE TO YOU?

"That's my baby," he responded, giving her a kiss on her lips.

Val's phone rung and it was the driver. She motioned for Bird, as he grabbed the rest of his belongings and they headed downstairs.

Val was nervous. She wanted everything to go as planned for the party. Her mother hasn't had a party in ages. Bird kept his hand rested on Val's knee the short ride to Ventana's. She leaned in and kissed him on the cheek so he would loosen up. She didn't need any problems with him or her family.

The driver opened the door. They both held hands entering the venue. She spotted her sister walking towards them and she heard Bird take a deep breath.

"Hey guys," she spoke, not looking at Bird. "People have started to arrive and everything is on point as planned. Uncle Junior is bringing her here and she thinks she's having dinner with a few friends. They'll arrive shortly," Shai noted before she walked off, as Val spotted the VIP table set aside for them, as she suggested.

She led Bird to the area which had a bottle of wine and champagne. Shai's boyfriend was already chilling.

"Sweetheart, I'll be back. Going to go over everything with Shai and the staff."

He nodded, reaching for his phone. Val rolled her eyes knowing he was in contact with Tyra. Before his phone locked, she read a text between the two earlier, as he laid it down to rush off to the bathroom. Tyra sent him a schedule of her son's basketball game, which confused her, but then it dawned on her that Bird had been spending time with her son, per their last conversation.

"Hello Auntie Pat," Val said giving her a huge hug.

"Girl I haven't seen you in forever and you stay right here in Atlanta. I hope that negro ain't keeping you away from your family," she said laughing, smearing lipstick on the side of Val's cheek.

"No, I'm sorry. I need to visit soon."

"Chile, I ain't going to hold my breath," she responded looking over in another direction leaving Val speechless, the she walked off.

Guests were entering as well as family members, who Val haven't seen in a while. She kept her eyes on Bird, to make sure he wasn't uncomfortable, but noticed he was engaged on his phone. She shook her head and then proceeded in making her rounds to each area greeting people. She saw one familiar face whose eyes happened to lock with hers.

The gentleman walked towards her direction. "Bret, thank you so much for coming, you look dapper," Val said welcoming him.

"Valerie, don't you look lovely," he responded, reaching in to give her a hug. They embraced, just as Shai ran over. "Uncle Junior and mom are pulling up now, let's get everybody in position!" she panicked.

"Sorry, Bret. I will get with you shortly," Val said and eased off. She turned back around to find Bird staring her down. She smiled and headed near the entrance.

"Everyone, simmer down. Mommy is about to come in. I need everyone quiet and yell surprise when she enters, okay?" Shai said to their guests.

"Okay," everyone said in unison.

Bird stood in the back, while everyone waited patiently. What felt like three minutes, felt more like ten. The doors open, "S-U-R-P-R-I-S-E!" everyone yelled and clapped.

Thelma's face was priceless. Tears started to form in her eyes, as she put her hand over her mouth. She was really surprised, as uncle Junior was glad to be a part of her big day.

"Oh mommy you look so beautiful!" Shai said.

"Girl your uncle said we were going to dinner and dancing with some of our childhood friends."

"You are, they are all here," Val chimed in.

"You guys really did good at keeping this from me. I appreciate both of you!" Thelma said giving her daughters hugs. "The decorations and the view is amazing, I'm so happy," she added.

"Anything for our queen," Val assured.

The DJ spun Earth, Wind, and Fire, as guests started greeting Thelma. She was very happy and pleased with everything and Val was happy. Val walked over to the drink station and ran into Bret again.

"What will you have?" he asked.

"A margarita on the rocks, nothing on the rim," she replied smiling.

WHO IS HE TO YOU?

"Now, don't forget about our lunch outing. I'll be in town all week."

"I'll be sure to add you on my schedule. Just let me know in advance," she agreed. "But on another note, I'm glad this party is finally over."

"Your mom looks great and very appreciative. This was nice of you guys to throw her a party. I sure miss my mother. She's been gone six years now."

"It doesn't seem like it's been that long since her passing. I remember. She was a nice and pretty lady."

Bret handed Val her margarita and she almost dropped it, as she noticed Bird walking up towards them.

"Sweetheart, I've been looking all over for you," he proclaimed. "What do we have here?" he asked looking at Val, then Bret.

"Hello, I'm Bret Smith. A longtime friend of Val," he said extending his hand out to Bird, who ignored it.

"Hello, I'm Omar Mize, Val's fiancé. Strange she never mentioned you, whatsoever," Bird added.

Sweat started to form on the top of Val's forehead. She was embarrassed and scared to open her mouth. Just then, Thelma and Shai walked up.

"Hi, Bret," Shai spoke.

"So everyone knows Bret except me?" Bird pointed out.

"Hello, Shai and Ms. Thelma. Happy Birthday. I'm so glad to be here to help you celebrate," Bret responded giving the ladies a hug. "If you all would excuse me," Bret conceded and walked away.

Val was uneasy. "What would you like to drink?" Bird asked Val.

"I have a margarita."

"You can put that one down, I'll get you another one."

"Val, baby, what was that all about?" Thelma asked.

"Nothing mom. Bret was just speaking to me and offered me a drink. I guess Bird is upset."

WHO IS HE TO YOU?

Bird turned around and cut his eyes at Val and her family. She did not want any problems. She was already uneasy and embarrassed. She really needed to apologize to Bret.

"Mom, go ahead and enjoy your party. Everything is good," Val said trying to ease Thelma's mind.

Thelma hissed as well as Shai. Thelma gave Bird an awful look and they both walked away. Val couldn't believe what just happened. Bird was so out of line. He stood like nothing bothered him. He tried giving Val her drink, but she refused. He sat it on the counter, unbothered.

"You guys did a good job on the party, and the staff as well," Bird stated. "So when were you going to introduce me to your lil' friend?"

"Bird, it's not a big deal. These are guests, people we know. Trust me, I'm not hiding anything from you, unlike you!" Val hissed back.

"What you mean by that?"

"You sat in the back the entire time, on your phone with your lil' girlfriend. Are you two planning an outing to her son's basketball game?" Val asked. "Why on earth would she be sending you her son's schedule?"

Confused, Bird didn't know what Val was talking about. He had to think about what she said. On the other hand, Val couldn't believe she told him what she knew.

"Did you go through my phone or something?" he asked Val, getting in her face. "Answer me!" he said louder, grabbing her arm.

"Hey now, I don't know what's going on, but you better take your hand off my niece!" Uncle Junior said, as Thelma and Shai came back running towards them, noticing the commotion.

"It's okay. We were having a slight disagreement, that's all," Val reassured her uncle and the rest of the on lookers, as Bird removed his hands and pulled Val closer to him.

"Put your hand on my daughter if you want to and it will be hell to pay, nigga! I promise you that!" Thelma growled in Bird's face.

"Mama, T, nothing is going on. Like Val said, we were having a slight disagreement. Please go enjoy your party," Bird said. He then turned to Val and whispered in her ear. "I'll be in the car downstairs and expect you to follow behind shortly. Love you." Bird kissed Val on the cheek and tried to kiss Thelma, who quickly pushed him away. Bird started laughing as if everything was funny.

Uncle Junior was disturbed and looked at Val. "Has he been hitting on you?"

"No, uncle Junior I'm fine, but thanks for being concerned."

"Mom I have to go. Everything is taken care of and paid for. I have a slight headache and need to go lay down. Please, go enjoy your guests," Val said in a rush, pleading with Thelma.

"You got to be kidding me? You are leaving because that asshole left?" Shai asked defensively.

"Shai, please not tonight. I have a headache."

"What you have is knots upside your head, from that asshole hitting on you! I can't believe you are leaving right now; my God we haven't even cut the cake!" Shai stated.

"Babygirl, I'm worried about you," Thelma admitted as she pleaded with Val to stay. "Please, come stay with me tonight."

"Mom, I'm so sorry. I have to meet Bird downstairs."

A tear fell from Thelma's eyes. She wanted desperately to help her daughter, who was way over her head with Bird. He had her wrapped around his fingers.

Shai motioned for the DJ to spin the music to something that would take the attention off of what was going on, as guests still looked on. "Mom, not here. Please don't cry," Shai whispered to Thelma.

"Val, when you leave, please stay away. Bird is where your heart is clearly at, nothing matters but him. We wish you the best!" Shai added and took her mom by the hand and left the area.

Val stood there speechless. She couldn't believe she was picking sides and going to leave her mom's party to meet Bird's needs. Not in a million years did she think she would be put in that position. She wanted badly to tell Bird to go to the hotel but didn't want to fight and was afraid of the consequences that would follow.

She finally was able to pick up her feet to move and started walking. She couldn't look at anyone and wished she could quietly sneak out. She spotted Bret talking to an unknown female and slowly eased by him.

WHO IS HE TO YOU?

Val didn't look back to see if people were looking at her. Once she made it out front, the driver opened her door for her to get in. Bird was awaiting her.

"Babe, the night is still young. Let's hit up Blue Flame," Bird said with a different attitude.

"The strip club?"

"Yes, maybe we both will get lucky tonight!" he winked.

Val was livid. Bird was making a mockery out of her and she had no control on what was happening around her.

CHAPTER TWELVE

V al woke up with a pounding headache. Her and Bird argued most of the night after he returned from the strip club. She was able to talk him into taking her back to the hotel. He wasn't pleased, but slightly pushed her out the car and had the driver drive off. Val had a bruise on her arm from hitting the pavement.

When Bird returned back to the room in the wee hours of the morning, he was drunk and wanted to have sex. Val knew if she refused, it would be a problem, so she gave in and got it over with. She faked orgasms after orgasms, so he would roll over and go to sleep. He did just that. What was supposed to be a wonderful night celebrating her mom's birthday, turned into a disaster.

Val didn't get the peaceful night she hoped for nor did she get a chance to put on the lingerie she brought. She looked over at Bird, who was snoring away. He looked peaceful sleeping, while she tossed and turned all night. Val got up and opened the door to the balcony overlooking the city. It was breezy, but comfortable. Val didn't realize how unhappy she was until the thought of jumping off the balcony crossed her mind. She looked down and then started tugging with her thoughts. Tears started to form and then she jumped at the sound of Bird's awakening voice.

"Val, sweetheart, what are you doing out there?"

Val wiped her eyes with her hands, "I'm just admiring the view."

"Come back to bed and admire this view. You got a whole man in here, who needs attention," Bird whined.

Just the thought of her giving anything or anyone her attention bothered him. Val rolled her eyes and let out a deep breath, then headed back inside to cuddle next to him. "Babe how was the club?" she asked out of curiosity.

"It was awesome and I'm sure you could tell because as soon as I got here, I wanted to dive right into you. You should have come along."

"The sex was kind of rough and you were drunk."

"I may have been tipsy, but not drunk! You came back to back, so I couldn't tell unless you were faking it and I know you wouldn't do that, now would you?"

Val was hesitant at first but went with the flow. "I have never!"

Bird squeezed Val's body as she lay next to him. She could still smell the alcohol on his breath but didn't say a word. Val glanced at the time and knew they had to get moving before checkout.

"Let's say we get out of here and go have brunch? I'm hungry and doubt any breakfast is left downstairs."

"Sounds good, you read my mind."

Val stood and dialed her mom's number as it rung and then a subscriber message was given to the caller. She then tried multiple times after and got the same message. Val then prompted to call Shai and the same message was given, "What the fuck?" she mumbled. Val started fuming. "I know they didn't change their numbers," she said to herself.

"Babe before we leave, I'd like to stop by my moms, her nor Shai's phone are working or they change their numbers."

"Sounds like a typical Shai move. Who needs them?" Bird said, "You got me, that's all that matters."

"They are my family! I hope me walking out on the party didn't cause problems."

"They want you all to themselves, that's all. If that's the case, fuck them all!" Bird said with no remorse.

Val was livid with Bird for speaking the way he was of her family and if Shai had her mother's number changed, she was in for a rude awakening. After forking out money for the party, I guess her job was done. Val already felt alienated with Bird, but now her family? She knew she had to speak with them as soon as possible; that's if they wanted to speak with her.

Val and Bird pulled up to her mother's house, just as she was getting out of Shai's car. They both looked back and locked eyes with one another. Val didn't know what that was all about, but she was hoping to find out.

Val got out the car, as Bird stayed behind just as his cell phone rang. Val was stuck in between trying to find out who the caller was on the other end with Bird and what her mom and Shai had going on.

The ladies sped up, as Val approached them, not acknowledging her presence. She knew something was up, when she noticed her mom's new cell phone.

"Are you guys mad with me or something?" Val blurted. "I tried to call both of you and the operator said the numbers had been changed," Val stated, confused.

"Valerie, sweetheart. Why are you here? I mean don't you need to go wipe Bird's ass?" Thelma said, nonchalantly.

Val was taken back with her mom's tone and choice of words. "Whoa, mom. I don't need to wipe anyone's ass; I came to check on you. Is this about the party?" Val asked defensive.

"The party was the last straw, it's everything else that's been building up. I will not sit around, watching you make a fool out of yourself and this family! That negro makes you look less of a woman and I didn't raise you that way, Valerie Taylor!"

"Bird has nothing to do with you acting this way. It's Shai, isn't it?"

WHO IS HE TO YOU?

"When my daughter comes back, bring her by! Until then, we will have nothing to do with you!" Thelma said, opening her screen door.

"Val, babe, hurry up. Let's go!" Bird said calling out from the car adding fuel to the fire.

Shai stood in the screen door, shaking her head.

Val turned her attention to Shai. "This is your entire fault! You've always been jealous of me, after all I've done for you, mom's birthday party, and y'all treat me like shit!" Val said angrily.

"Val, I've never been jealous of you or your relationship. I think you should leave, you heard your master, he's ready to go!" she shot back and slammed the front door.

Val jumped. The sound of the door stung. She was livid and felt alienated. She knew her mom was upset after she left her party, but not to the point to cut her out of her life. She hated she had to leave; she just didn't want to cause any problems with Bird.

Val got in the car, looking back noticing someone peeping out the window as tears ran down her face. Bird put one hand on Val's knee and then drove off.

"Baby, you don't need them. Family is just as bad as anybody, you know that."

"Bird, that's my family! Had we not stormed out of the party; everything would be fine! Damn!" Val cried out.

"Don't your ass go blaming me! They bougie asses never liked me from the get-go. You see all they trying to do is cause problems between us. Fuck your old ass momma and jealous ass sister. She just mad because she can't get this dick!" Bird said with anger.

"Excuse me? Shai don't want you and my momma isn't old! Watch your mouth!" she shot back.

"Or what? What you gone do, Val? Shai been trying to get this dick, I just never said nothing."

Val buried her head in her lap, trying to figure out what Bird was talking about with Shai and what was going on around her. She wanted desperately to push Bird out the vehicle and keep going, but then she'd be a dead woman.

Val couldn't control her tears and couldn't wait to get home. She quickly popped a Xanax. The weekend was supposed to be an amazing one but end up being nothing but pure hell. Bird didn't have a care in the world. He seemed to be enjoying what was going on.

CHAPTER THIRTEEN

A Few Months Later…

Val finally returned home from the hospital, after suffering a miscarriage. Everything in her life seemed to have been falling apart. She hasn't talked to her family in months. It seems like every day was getting worse by the day, her life, job, and relationship with Bird, who caused her to have a miscarriage in the first place.

Val caught Bird with Tyra and her son at the movies and confronted him. Bird demanded Val take her pregnant ass home and not worry about what he was doing. Instead she caused a scene, in which Tyra took her son and left the area, when Bird arrived home that night, she caught every blow it was, leaving her in a corner trying to protect her unborn child. Bird kicked her in the side, bruised her entire body, most of all losing her child. Bird tried to make light of the situation, to keep Val from pressing charges and stated they would try for another baby again soon.

WHO IS HE TO YOU?

Val walked into the bedroom and noticed every floral arrangement there was and a big teddy bear. She stood as the room seemed to have been spinning, she almost fell as her knees locked and Bird caught her.

"Sweetheart let me help you," Bird said, helping Val to a chair and propped her feet up. "I need you to rest and I mean rest. You've been through a lot."

Val was hurt, because he was the reason she was in that place. The one man she thought she could count on and thought he wanted a baby just as bad as she did. The thought of the doctors telling her they couldn't hear a heartbeat made her sick to her stomach. She cried like a newborn baby. Bird was doing his best trying to comfort her. He knew it was his fault, but didn't want to admit it, not even the bruises on her body she wore.

With everything that was going on in Val's life, she was forced to step down at work, in which Emily took on most of Val's duties. At this rate, Val was wondering why Marc was still holding on to her. He didn't care for her, but knew deep down, he knew much more than what he was saying. Tyra resigned a few weeks ago, but that didn't stop her relationship with Bird. Every time she gets the urge of leaving, something draws her back in. She wanted so desperately to reach out to someone to see if it was a mental thing or just a control thing. Bird would be so nice and so loving, then he'd flip so eagerly without knowing it. Val often wondered if he treated Tyra the same way. She knew how he treated Chanel.

"Val, what would you like to eat?"

"Maybe a salad, something light. I'm not really hungry."

"How about I pick you up a salad from your favorite place, Texas Roadhouse?"

"Sounds really good, with everything on it."

"I'll go ahead and call in dinner and go pick it up."

Val didn't care; she needed a few moments alone. Spending two days in the hospital was not what she needed. Her body was still in so much pain. As soon as she heard Bird leave, she burst out into tears. She knew what she was experiencing wasn't love, but why couldn't she leave? After a few minutes of feeling sorry for herself, she logged onto Facebook from her phone and typed in domestic violence groups. She found several, but only joined two. Val never really posted on social media, but always scrolled her newsfeed to see what people were up to. She noticed her family also unfriended her. She held back more tears and clicked on the 'Domestic Violence support for women group' and entered. Val was curious to see what other women in her situation were going through and started reading the posts. Some of the posts made her mad, some were downright awful and some put her at ease, knowing there was hope. Val couldn't believe some of the posts she read. She knew if she stayed it would only get worse. Val started to comment on one of the posts until her phone rang.

"Hello, Emily. It's so good to hear from you. How are you?"

"The question is how are you?"

"I'm actually okay. I haven't been home that long from the hospital, but it's a process."

"Val, please come and stay with me for a while. I know you like your space, but I am more than your co-worker, and I worry about you. A man that continuously beats you and makes you miscarry is a dirty dog! You deserve better, heck get a restraining order," she begged.

"Emily it's not that simple. It's easier said than done and you know he will hunt me down," Val spoke in between sniffs. "I'll be okay, I'm finding support."

"Val, you've lost your family, your unborn baby, and your job is hanging by a thread. It seems like you're locked up in a cage. That's not love, sweetheart. Pretty soon, he's going to stop all contacts, including me!"

"That won't happen. You're all I have left at this moment. I'm trying to get the strength to return back to work, pretty soon."

Emily protested, "I hope you don't mind, but I kind of talked to Marc and stated you were going through a lot of personal issues, you were afraid to speak to him about. Although he heard the rumors about Tyra, he felt bad and decided to keep a job for you available. I didn't give him a lot of info, just enough so he wouldn't terminate you."

"Emily, that wasn't necessary, but thanks. At this point I care, but I don't care," Val revealed. "People talking about me, my family has alienated me out of their lives and I got a man who claims he loves me so much, that nothing I do satisfies him. I'm catching blows instead! What is there to live for?" Val calmly stated through the phone, while holding her stomach.

"Please, Val don't talk like that. I'm only trying to help. I'm here for you. Please let me help you?" Emily pleaded.

WHO IS HE TO YOU?

Val was crying uncontrollably and didn't realize Bird had come in. He ran over to her and grabbed the phone out her hand.

"Hello, who's speaking?"

"This is Emily, is Val okay?"

"Yes, she needs some rest and you're upsetting her," Bird said and hung up. He then noticed Val was on Facebook in a Domestic Violence Group and wondered what that was about. He deactivated her page and turned her phone off.

"Babe, I need you to rest. You can talk to Emily later, she's upsetting you," Bird hinted. He stayed close to Val and gave her a sedative to help her rest. He didn't want anyone close to her telling her what to do. He was beginning to think Val didn't need a job and could stay home, but he knew Val was independent and wouldn't go for that.

"Please don't leave me," Val said between slurs. She wanted to be loved deeply by the one man, who couldn't love her back in return.

Bird knew in his heart, he was hurting Val, and the loss of their baby made it worse. He knew he had a problem, but every time he got upset, he took it out on her. He just wanted to have a great life and that required having his son, Tyler in his life. He looked at the photos he retrieved from the mail and added them in his phone. He was happy to see how big his son has gotten. He had no idea how Chanel got their address to send the photos, nor was there a return address on the postage, he was just glad she sent him something reassuring him his son was okay.

He wished he could reconcile with Chanel and make things right. He just wanted to be a good father to his kid and not spending time with someone else's child. Bird looked over at Tyra and how peaceful she was, only to still feel empty inside. He didn't love her the way he loved Val but didn't understand why he couldn't let go either. Although business was great for them both, especially Tyra's charity, he thought he would step back slowly, so he wouldn't hurt her. Tyra was pushing for him to leave Val completely, so they'd be a family, but he didn't love her like that. He only fucked with Tyra because it was easy and the more and more he did it, it became a habit.

Bird put on his clothes, trying not to wake Tyra. She had fallen asleep soon after he dicked her down. Tyra was not a woman who needed a man; she could function without Bird, one thing he disliked. He needed Tyra to need him. He almost tripped stepping on her shoes and hit his toe on the edge of the bed.

"Shit!" he hollered.

Tyra awakened, looking around the room and locked eyes with Bird.

"Where are you going? You haven't been here that long," she asked.

"I'm going to head out a little early. I need to get back to Val, given what's she's been through," he replied.

"What about me? I had a miscarriage too, let's not forget," she added.

"I was there for you, too. Let's not forget," he said, looking for his shoes. "Sweetheart, Val doesn't have any kids and this miscarriage took a toll on her. Let's not argue."

"Who's arguing? I'm just saying I need you too."

Bird kept moving accordingly. He didn't want to have to get into it with Tyra about nonsense. She wasn't his focus at the moment and he sure didn't care how she felt. He knew if he gave into her, she would rub it in Val's face. He needed to try and distance himself from that entire situation, after he gets his threesome.

"Babe I got to bounce. I promise, when Val is feeling better, we all will get together, and this won't be a problem anymore."

"Like hell, I'm not fucking Val!" Tyra reassured him.

Bird rushed over and kissed Tyra, so he could leave, instead she pushed him away. He didn't want any problems, he politely left. Bird heard Tyra cursing him out the door. He laughed on his way to his car. He wasn't about to deal with her bullshit. He stopped by, got what he wanted and decided to leave. Bird knew one thing for sure, Tyra had some good pussy, even if it came with a price. The better the pussy, the crazier the woman!

He backed out the driveway and headed out her subdivision. He decided on the way home, he would try and do right by Val. He had issues and knew that, but the one woman that's always been by his side, was at home waiting on him. Bird stopped by the store and picked up some roses, hoping that would uplift Val and a bottle of sparkling cider. He didn't want anything, but he needed Val to forget what happened and make it right.

Bird was surprised, when he got home. Val was up and working on her computer. He thought she'd be resting.

"Sweetheart, these are for you," he said presenting her with the roses.

She beamed, "Thanks."

"How are you feeling?"

"I'm still a little weak, but I'm feeling better for the most part. I decided to get something's done, then sitting around going crazy."

"I'm glad you aren't laying around feeling sorry for yourself,' he said, but it didn't come out right. "I'm sorry, I didn't mean it that way."

"Let's not forget how this all happened in the first place!" Val snapped back. She was shaking, while putting a hand on her forehead.

Bird walked over toward Val, as she jumped. She was so afraid of him; she didn't know what he may do.

She wasn't able to fight back, she was drained. Instead, He kneeled to where she was sitting and hugged her. He kissed her forehead and took her by the face. "I'm so sorry. Sorry that I put you and our baby through this. I never meant for any of this to happen."

Val was still shaking but embraced him anyway. She looked him in the eyes and wanted to believe him, but knew it was a cycle. His actions always reverted to hitting her and she didn't deserve that. She was too afraid to look away.

"We'll try again, soon. We are meant to be."

"Babe, I'm not sure if I want to try anytime soon. I think I am over this baby thing, maybe in the future."

Bird stood up looking at Val like she was crazy. He didn't know how to react to her statement.

"Like hell!' he responded. He thought all along, Val wanted to bare his child, but now she was stating otherwise. "Please, don't let that miscarriage rip us apart, Val! I deserve a baby from you!"

She knew that look and the way he was talking, made her change her tone. Val knew getting pregnant by him again wasn't wise. "I agree, Bird, you do deserve a child, I'm not sure if I would be a great mother, that's all!" she retracted, trying to rectify the situation.

"Val you would be an amazing mother, it's me." He pulled out the photos of Tyler and presented them to Val. "Chanel sent these to me in the mail, with no return address of course, not sure how she got our address, but I'm just glad to see him. Look at how big he's gotten."

Val almost sunk in her chair, knowing she gave Chanel their address. She just hoped staying in contact with Chanel would not backfire. She looked at the photos and saw Bird all over Tyler, he was a spitting image of his father. She noticed the tears in Bird's eyes and couldn't help but wonder how good of a father he would be.

"I'll have your baby, Mr. Mize!" Val beamed just seeing how he reacted to Tyler's photos, hoping a baby would change him for the better.

"Soon, baby, soon! Thank you!"

They locked lips with one another, just as happy as a couple should be. Val knew life could only get better from that moment. She knew, Chanel would eventually come around soon, at least she hoped.

CHAPTER FOURTEEN

Things were going good for Val and Bird for the most part. A few weeks in and the couple couldn't be happier. Val was getting the attention and affection she needed, and they managed to sneak in a few dates. She was glowing, and her coworkers noticed. Marc slacked off and wasn't giving her a hard time, plus Tyra wasn't working there anymore, which made things better. Val promised to give Bird his threesome with Tyra. He promised after they got together he was done with her for good. Val knew that wasn't something she really wanted to do, but if that makes him happy, then she'll follow through on her word. Tyra was coming over later, so Val wanted to rush home and prepare, she hoped it put an end to their relationship.

"What's up sweet pea, are you dipping out early?" Derrick asked.

"Hey, sugar. Yes, I am as a matter of fact. Got something planned," Val responded with a smile on her face.

WHO IS HE TO YOU?

"Oh, I wasn't invited."

"Neither was I, so don't feel bad Derrick," Emily chimed in, walking toward the two.

"I'll let you two chat. I'll catch up with you tomorrow, lady. Have fun," Derrick said and walked off.

"I was coming over to invite you to dinner, but I see you got plans. What you got going on?" Emily asked being nosey.

"A little something with my man. I promised him an amazing evening," Val replied winking at Emily.

"Oh, sounds good. What is it, besides sex?" she said laughing.

"Ha-ha…a threesome!"

"Whatever girl, now you are tripping," Emily said, while noticing the look on Val's face and then looked around the room. "You are kidding right?"

Val leaned in, "The only way to end this affair with Bird and Tyra is to join them!"

"Now you sound like a fool! I knew everything was too good to be true. These couple of weeks you've been on cloud nine, now he talked you into a threesome! Whew girl, that dick is a hell of a drug!" Emily responded, getting pissed. She forgot where she was.

"Sheesh, please. It was my decision. We talked about it for some time now and I'm ready."

"Girl, you are really fucked up. Excuse my French, but that isn't ever going to stop a man from stepping outside the box. I did any and everything for my ex-husband and he still ran over me."

"Look I got to go. I'll fill you in later. I don't have time to go back and forth with you." Val grabbed her things and excused herself; as Emily stood back looking on in disbelief.

"What was that all about?" Derrick walked back up and asked.

Emily looked at him with tears in her eyes. "She's losing it," and walked off.

Val didn't want anyone judging her or the decisions she made. She should have kept her mouth shut! On the other hand, Val was rushing out to get a fresh wax and head home to get herself together before

WHO IS HE TO YOU?

Tyra arrived. She didn't know what to expect and the experience. She was about to do something totally out the norm and prayed this brought her and Bird closer. She was ready to start their family and she told him after tonight that would happen.

When Val arrived home, Bird had dinner ready. She hurried and showered, so she could eat and let her food digest. Bird could tell she was nervous. He put his hand on her shoulders, "Relax, babe. There is nothing to be nervous about."

She took a drink of her wine, so it could ease her a little. "What time, ole girl coming over?"

Bird laughed because Val hasn't talked like that in a long time. "She'll be over in about an hour she said." Bird glanced over and smiled. "I think you need this more than I do."

"Remember, this is for you, not me."

"Us, remember us."

She shook her head. Bird prepared grilled chicken, a salad, and asparagus. Val didn't usually eat much, so she ate lite because she knew she was about to burn some calories. As soon as they were done eating, Bird cleaned the kitchen and pulled Val close to him. Just him gazing into her eyes, made her melt. She loved those moments and never wanted to see the ugly side of him again. Bird was the most attractive man to her. His caramel mocha skin and fit body was perfect. Bird had a mole next to his left eye that stood out, that was his signature. As they enjoyed their few moments together, the doorbell rang. Val took a deep breath, letting go of Bird so he could answer the door.

Her anxiety started to kick in as she was starting to sweat. She took deep breaths and headed to the living room area. She noticed Tyra with a shorter hairdo and her red lips. This Tyra, looked as though she was ready to put it down, not the workplace diva. Val put on a fake smile, as Bird closed the door, while Tyra walked towards her. Before Val could utter a word, Tyra smiled and then proceeded to kiss her on her lips.

"Hello, Val. Long time no see," Tyra stepped back and said.

"You look great," was all Val could manage to say.

"Tyra, please follow Val to the bedroom," Bird ordered, as he slapped Tyra on the ass.

Val didn't say a word. She led while both followed, entering the bedroom her and Bird shared.

WHO IS HE TO YOU?

Tyra looked around; she glanced at a painting hanging on the wall and looked stunned.

"Nice art, I dig it," she said.

"Thanks. Bird had it made and delivered from Paris."

"Ladies let's get undressed, so we can get this show on the road," Bird said, not wanting to waste any time.

He looked over at Val, who was struggling. He knew she was uncomfortable, but he needed her to get it together. He decided to pour them all a drink to loosen up.

Everyone took a drink of the Hennessey Bird poured. Tyra smiled at him, then proceeded to run her hand across Bird's chest. She started to help him undress as Val stood back, not knowing how to react. Bird watched Val in the background looking on as he fondled Tyra. She stopped and motioned for Bird to get on the bed and advised Val to do the same.

Val took the rest of the drink to the head and shook it off. She then climbed on the bed butt naked next to Bird waiting on instructions.

"Val I'm going to need you to seduce our man," Tyra ordered.

"Excuse me, my man!" Val shot back.

"Whatever," Tyra said, knowing Val was in denial.

Val climbed on top of Bird, who was already in position, and started planting kisses on him. Val ran her tongue across Bird's muscular, yet hairy chest and then onto his nipples. Bird picked her head up, pulled her close and deep throated her. He squeezed Val's ass, getting her wet. Bird stopped and directed her to his erection, as she eased down and put her warm mouth on it, slurping up and down his shaft. He grabbed her by the head, pushing her up and down, moaning to her rhythm. He looked up and watched Tyra in the background. He knew she was getting aroused but couldn't help but to direct himself back to Val who took all his balls in at one time, making him want to cum in her mouth. His eyes rolled to the back of his head in pleasure.

"Oh, my goodness, that feels so good," Val let out causing Bird to open his eyes, noticing Tyra, who had Val's butt cheeks wide open sucking every drip of wetness out of her. Bird watched Val's every facial expression, body language and knew she was enjoying Tyra's tongue. He started masturbating, watching the pair. Tyra was a hell of a woman pleaser and knew she was going to turn Val out. Tyra face was buried in Val's ass, sticking her tongue in her anus, bringing it to her vagina. She sucked on her clit, as Val was beginning to shake with so much pleasure.

"Turn on your back," Tyra instructed Val.

Val turned around and spread eagle, as Bird decided to watch the pair in action. Tyra took her time with Val, forgetting they ever worked together and gently took her titties in one by one. Val had some nice perky titties and it showed. Tyra fingered her, making her even wetter as she tongue kissed her. The pair shared a passionate kiss and Bird couldn't tell if that was Val's first girl experience or not. Val took one of Tyra's titties in her mouth, as she let loose and went downtown on her. Her mouth felt good on her clitoris and she eased her tongue in and out her pussy. Val was getting wetter and wetter as she kissed and sucked her making her clinch. Bird had enough and decided to enter Tyra from the back pushing in and out of her. It felt so good, he had to stop and eat her out to keep from cumming. She moaned in pleasure, as she pleased Val. The trio was in paradise. Bird resumed and fucked Tyra until she started to shake.

"That's right daddy, go deeper," Tyra managed to say.

Val looked at the pair and could tell their bodies were in sync with each other. She was disappointed to see Bird wasn't wearing a condom as he fucked her, putting her and his life at risk, knowing that's how they got down. She watched her man eat Tyra's pussy and fuck her, so she decided to play the same game once he came. Bird on the other hand, squeezed Tyra soft, fat ass and pulled out just in time, as he came in the crack of her ass. He loved watching it drip onto the sheets.

"Damn, I needed that. You got some bomb ass pussy," Bird said to Tyra, as if Val wasn't in the room. He got up from the bed to clean himself off.

Val flipped Tyra over and went to work on her. She sat on Tyra's face, riding her like a G4, letting her catch every drop of juice she had left. Val pleased Tyra so good, making Bird catch an eyeful. He stood in the back, looking on holding his dick. Val went down on her, sucking all Tyra's and Bird's juices. Tyra rocked along to Val's rhythm, making love to her as she ate her out. Val felt her cum as she begged her to come up and felt her body shiver as she then slid her tongue in and out of her.

Val came up and kissed her passionately, while rubbing her breast. "I've never felt that before, that was different," Tyra whispered in Val's ear.

WHO IS HE TO YOU?

"Felt what?" Val asked, not knowing what she had done.

"That orgasm was everything. Not even Bird could make it rock like that," she replied as they both giggled.

"That was a nice little scene. The way you both were in tune with each other, got me feeling some type of way," Bird stated.

"I'm going to shower; can you show me to your bathroom?" Tyra asked.

Val pointed her in the right direction. Once she was out of the room, she looked at Bird, wanting more. He seemed tired. "Babe, I'm wore out," he proclaimed. "You sure you and Tyra haven't secretly been together before?"

"No, this was my first experience. I must admit, I really enjoyed it."

"I knew you would, seems like you enjoyed it a little too much."

Not sure what that meant, Val poured herself a drink and headed to the shower where Tyra was. She sat the drink down on the console table and opened the door, letting herself in. Tyra was waiting on Val as she welcomed her into the warm waters, spreading her legs apart, stooping under the shower head kissing her below. Val had never felt so good and by a woman at that. She put her head back against the wall letting the water hit her in the face. The adrenalin from the alcohol was kicking in, along with Tyra slithering ass tongue. She came up and they locked lips fingering each other. Val squeezed her ass not realizing the shower door was open, until she felt some cold air. She noticed Bird standing, watching them with his dick hung over.

"This get together is over! Tyra please hurry and go home! Val please go shower in the other room," he announced.

"Babe, what's going on?" Tyra asked.

"Just do what I say."

Val hurried and got her ass out the shower and went into the other bathroom. Bird slammed the shower door on Tyra and began to feel a rage coming over him, noticing how both of his ladies were enjoying each other and not him. It was him, who brought them together. He knew after tonight he was going to lay some ground rules down and make sure they never cross paths again, unless he insists!

CHAPTER FIFTEEN

Tyra didn't know what was going on because her and Bird have had several threesomes, but nothing like Val. She wouldn't have never thought her and Val would end up feeling each other. Tyra left a message for Val to meet her at her place during lunch, knowing Bird would be busy and wouldn't be looking for her.

Tyra noticed how scared Val was around Bird but couldn't put her finger on it. She had heard rumors in the past at the workplace that Bird might be putting his hands on her, but he has never showed her that side of him besides that one time at their event and she put his ass in check. Ever since then, he hasn't budged.

Tyra was putting her finishing touch on the chicken salad she was making, in case Val hadn't eaten. All she wanted to do was suck the girl's juices and feed her at the same time, was that too much to ask? She enjoyed their conversations over text and couldn't wait to see her. As she finished, she heard three knocks on the door.

Tyra washed and dried her hands, then made her way to answer the door. She was glad to see Val's face. She walked in leaving her shoes at the door.

"I'm glad you could make it. It's been awhile since our last encounter," Tyra said.

"I know, I know. I've been thinking about you, isn't that crazy?" she replied.

"The crazy part is our love for the same man, yet we used to work together and never had any dealings with each other," Tyra responded. She looked over at Val, who was admiring her son's photo.

"He's handsome, Tyra. He must look like his dad?"

"Naw, hoe, he favors his mama!" Tyra said jokingly as they both laughed. "On the real, he favors him a little and for the record that's not Bird's son," she added.

Val kept admiring the photo, which was weird to Tyra. "What about you, you want kids?"

"Sure, one day. I recently had a miscarriage. Bird and I decided to try again."

WHO IS HE TO YOU?

"Oh, really?" Tyra said acting surprised. "I mean, I'm sorry to hear, Bird never mentioned it, at all."

"Why would he? He's a liar and a cheater, whose playing the both of us, yet I still remain by his side."

"If it makes you feel any better, I'm in the same boat, as his side chic. Let's beat him at his own game."

What Tyra didn't understand is that playing with Bird, would only backfire and she would be the one catching his blows. Val wasn't about to dig a bigger hole; she was already taking a chance by coming over to her place.

Val took a bite of her sandwich Tyra had placed in front of her. It was a hell of a chicken salad sandwich.

"How is it?" Tyra asked.

"It's tasty, very good."

"Well when you get done eating, allow me to seduce you, too!" Tyra said, as she brushed up against Val. She was way over her head. She couldn't believe her threesome turned into a twosome, that didn't include Bird. She knew it would be a mistake granting him his request but thought it would be the other way around.

She had no intentions, whatsoever, of forming a bond with his mistress. She told Emily what was going on and that was a mistake. Emily hasn't spoke to her in a few days. Emily thinks it's a fluke that all of a sudden, Tyra wants her to herself.

Val thought about it but didn't think that was the case at all. She wanted to see if she stayed close to Tyra, if it would end things with Bird. She was so deep in thought, that she didn't hear Tyra calling out for her. She finished her sandwich and club soda, and then made her way to her bedroom, which was lit with bath and bodyworks candles, her favorite; Lavender.

Tyra was in a red teddy, with her ass out. Val noticed the shots on the table and decided to take a few to the head. That would definitely get her in the mood, for this girl on girl adventure. She removed her dress, revealing her freshly waxed pussy and erect nipples, making her way to the bed. Val didn't want to waste time, since she needed to be on her way home. She didn't want to be out of Bird's sight for way too long. Val made her way to Tyra, making eye contact. They kissed passionately. Val started helping Tyra get her teddy off, so she could make love to her.

Val started planting kisses on her. She took her breasts in one by one, making circular motions around her nipple. As Val sucked on her, her hand made her way to her clitoris and she rubbed it, easing her way down to her wetness. Tyra moaned as her hips thrust in motion. Val let up, then made her way to her wetness and stuck her tongue in Tyra's pussy. She began licking her slowly. Tyra moaned in awe. Val continued with a rhythm by slurping, licking and sucking. She stuck a finger in Tyra's anus and then slid her tongue from her pussy to her butthole.

"Oh, Val, that feels amazing!" Tyra whispered.

"I was taught by the best, you taste amazing, too," Val replied, gripping Tyra's ass, as she lifted her and brought her pussy closer to eat her out.

When Val first stepped into the room, her heart was pounding, as she was about to have a one on one fuck session with the woman, who had her man's heart. She knew Bird felt strongly about Tyra, or else he wouldn't keep bringing her in their lives, now the table has turned.

Tyra pulled Val up to kiss her, as Tank was playing in the background. She turned Val over and immediately went down on her. Val didn't notice the whip cream, until Tyra shook it up and start putting it in her pussy. She jumped with the coldness of the cream.

BIANCA HARRISON

"Relax, baby. This is going to feel real good." Tyra whispered. She took a piece of menthol in her mouth, as she started licking the cream out of Val. The cool breeze and warmness of her mouth, made Val trembled; she has never felt anything like that before. Tyra went deeper in Val until she licked all of the cream out of her.

Once up for air, Tyra strapped on a strap on dildo, so she could enter Val.

Val was hesitant as first but decided to go with the flow. She let Tyra have her way and fuck her with the dildo, making her cum instantly.

"My God, you are the truth! I haven't trembled and shaken like that in a long time, not even with Bird."

"That's why we're here. Our first encounter was amazing, but this moment is even better," Tyra added. "I figured you would enjoy the experience more, without Bird in the background."

"I did! I was scared to come, but glad I did. It felt great."

The two rubbed on each other and kissed some more. Val didn't have a clue what she was doing or setting herself up for, but that orgasm was everything.

WHO IS HE TO YOU?

She started climbing on top of Tyra, kissing her passionately as they continued to kiss.

As the music played and skipped over to Teddy Pendergrass, Tyra heard a noise only to look up and notice someone standing in the doorway. Her adrenaline sped up.

"Bird is that you?" she quickly asked.

Val paused, in terror as her eyes got big.

Bird appeared with a beer can in tow walking out the shadows towards the bed.

"How did you get in here? I took my key back!" Tyra asked.

"You ladies seemed to have gotten closer. I enjoyed that little performance you both put on back there. Valerie I didn't know you had it in you."

"Baby I can explain," Val muffled, trying to ease out the bed.

"Bitch, get your clothes on and get home now!" he demanded, while Val jumped to her feet looking for her clothes. She was beyond terrified.

"Bird, watch your mouth! You don't talk to her like that!" Tyra chimed in. "Val you don't have to go, he's leaving!"

Val ignored her, getting dressed. Bird was obviously a little tipsy; he couldn't stand straight.

"Both of my bitches getting it in I see. My dick got extra hard watching you two. I must admit I created a beautiful thing between you two."

Tyra grabbed her robe, getting agitated. "Bird you need to leave, now!" she hollered.

"Or what? What you gone do, Tyra?" he said. "You were only good for a piece of ass, now you after my wife?"

Before Tyra knew it, she slapped the shit out of Bird.

"You fucking, bitch!" he said holding his face.

Val brushed passed the two, grabbed her things and left, fearing what was to come for her later. She wanted to help Tyra, so bad, but was afraid. She hurried to her car, praying Tyra could handle him on her own. Val prayed that Bird's appearance was not planned, thinking back to Emily's comment. She hoped Tyra wouldn't have betrayed her but kept wrestling with Emily's words in the back of her mind, now her life was in jeopardy.

Val was at home pacing the floor in a panic. She had drunk some vodka just to deal with Bird once he arrived. She didn't know what was taking him so long. She kept checking her phone and nothing. She wanted to call Tyra but figured that would be a mistake. She did dial Emily on her way home, trying to make sense of what just happened.

Emily pissed Val off so bad, she ended up hanging up on her. She knew Emily meant well, but she couldn't deal with her *I told you so* lecture.

Val just needed Emily's ear, not her opinions. She took another drink, just as she heard Bird unlock the door. They both made eye contact and Val's heart started beating faster. He walked in looking drenched; she can only imagine what happened between him and Tyra. He walked towards her looking pissed.

"How could you betray me? Sleep with my bitch, behind my back? I could have brought her here, if you wanted her that bad!" Bird said, as he took off his shirt and threw it on the floor. He started unbuckling his belt and his pants hit the floor.

"Baby I can explain! I'm sorry, but your bitch wanted me. She lured me over there, it wasn't supposed to go down like that," she pleaded.

"Is that so? So you just happen to fall in her pussy face first? Oh I watched you in the background as you got down, you lying whore!" Bird replied, slapping Val into the wall. "Don't you ever disrespect me like that again! That's my pussy, you hear me? Do you fucking hear me?" he asked standing in front of Val, as spit hit her nose.

Val cried as she held her face, "Yes, I hear you! You said you weren't going to hit me, again!"

"I said a lot of things, but you betrayed me and I didn't like how you were enjoying Tyra. Look like you enjoyed her more than me and that, I didn't like! The way you kissed her, made love to her, nearly made me sick!"

Val was hesitant to speak, as he had betrayed her their entire relationship by cheating on her but was now trying to call her out about doing the same. "Baby I'm so sorry! What more do you want?"

WHO IS HE TO YOU?

He grabbed her by her neck and looked her in her eyes as she tried to remove his hand. "What more do I want? I want you to fuck me, better than you did Tyra. I need you on your knees, like now!" He said with so much fear, that made Val drop to her knees as his grip loosened around her neck. Tears were falling as she pulled down his briefs and began sucking. His balls smelled just like Tyra. Val knew her scent. She cried even more knowing he just fucked the woman she was with and thought Tyra would have left him alone after today.

"Wipe them damn tears up! I don't need you crying while sucking me."

Val almost gagged, but had to hold it in. He kept grabbing her by her hair, pushing his head in making her suck harder.

"That's right baby that feel so good, that mouth of yours is everything," he whispered, pushing his dick in and out of her mouth as she got tired. He looked down at Val, as he was about to bust a nut. "Baby I'm about to cum," he said. Val was about to let up, instead he pulled out and released all in her face, hair, and neck as his semen started to drip. Val was pissed.

"Don't move," he demanded. Val's knees we're about to lock and give out, while the tears began to fall, as she looked like a drenched cum poster. He shook the rest of his sperm off on to her and then laughed like something was funny. "That's for being a naughty, bitch! Now go clean your nasty looking ass up! I don't need your pussy; I just had some before I pushed my dick in your mouth!"

Val began to stand, holding on to the wall to keep her balance from being on her knees too long. Her mind was all over the place as she felt like she'd been played. She finally got to the bathroom and couldn't even look at herself in the mirror. She immediately turned on the shower, removed her clothes and jumped in, crying under the shower head. She reached for her shampoo and washed her hair and any part of Bird off of her, Val finally had enough. She scrubbed her body until the water got cold.

She dried herself off and slipped on a pair of lounging pants and a T-shirt followed by her slide-ins. She quickly blow dried her hair and threw on a hat. She quietly opened the door, looking for Bird. He was in the kitchen looking in the refrigerator.

Val's voice was hoarse and trembled as she opened her mouth, "Baby I'm going to run out to the store to get more shampoo and some dinner, if that's okay with you?"

He closed the fridge, looking her up and down. He took a sip of his drink. "UberEATS is available right? I have shampoo, why the need to go out?"

"I like to use my own shampoo and barely had enough to wash my hair. It's not completely clean," she lied.

He walked over, knocking Val's hat off her head. "Your hair looks fine to me. I'll pick you some up tomorrow. I'm hungry, now."

Bird turned around and walked back toward the refrigerator. Val quickly grabbed her keys and purse on the counter, running towards the front door. She was struggling to get the deadbolt open. The door open and she was relieved, just as she felt a hand tugging her on her shirt. Val started to scream, "Help! Help! Please help me!" she called out for someone to hear her, as Bird dragged her by her shirt, finally able to put his hands over her mouth.

He finally got Val back inside the house and locked the door. "Are you trying to leave me? You ain't going nowhere, you hear me?" he yelled, and then hit her upside her head. She finally hit him back and that surprised him. She feared for her life as she sat back on the couch.

"You hit me?" He went back towards Val, hitting her in her chest, she could barely breathe. She kicked him and tried her best to fight him off. He hit her, she hit him back, she kicked him in the groin and he yelled in agony. "You bitch!" He charged her, and she was able to grab her keys and sprayed her mace in his face.

"Ouch! What the fuck!"

She ran towards the door, again. This time something struck her in the back and she fell to her knees. "You ain't going anywhere!" Bird said standing over her with a bat.

"Noooo, Bird!" she yelled as he hit her repeatedly with the bat, kicked her in her face, stood over her and punched her, as she had to ball in a fetal position and cover her head, but the blows kept coming. Bird began to stomp her face, Val couldn't hear her own cries, his last blow struck her in her chest so hard.

"To death do us part, sweetheart! I told you, you ain't going anywhere, you mine forever!" were the last words Valerie Taylor remembered.

CHAPTER SIXTEEN

What Is Love?

Val was conscious, but was in so much pain, as she suffered a broken nose, a fractured cheekbone, missing teeth and a concussion, which caused her to have a few seizures. She also had bruises all over her body, a bruised kidney and a damaged liver. Her chest was tight and she could barely breathe, when she noticed Bird walking towards her.

He leaned in and whispered in Val's ear, "You hurt yourself, remember that and you'll live."

Val was frightened. He stepped back as a nurse walked in and noticed her vital signs were off.

"Ms. Taylor, are you okay? Your blood pressure is extremely high," she looked over at Bird, who stood off in the background and then turned back around to face Val. "Please calm down. I'm going to have to call the doctor in, so we can get your blood pressure stabilized."

Bird stood on the side with a finger pressed over his lips to let Val know, if she opened her mouth, he would kill her.

As the nurse paged the station, Emily rushed in and Bird jumped.

"What is this bitch doing here?" he mumbled to himself.

She ran over to Val. "Oh my God!" she said, as she puts her hand over her mouth, noticing her face and the machines she was hooked up to. She hugged her friend and then wiped a tear from her face.

As the doctor walks in, the nurse approaches Emily. "May I ask? What's your relationship to the patient?"

"I'm sorry, I'm her best friend," she responds. She sights Bird, slinging her purse at him. "You bastard! You want to fight a woman? Fight me then!" she yelled as she lunged at him.

The doctor ran over and pulled Emily off of Bird.

Bird had a smirk on his face the entire time. "You are delusional! Ask Val what happened!" he said.

WHO IS HE TO YOU?

"He almost killed her! Look at her," Emily said to the nurse and doctor. "I spoke to a friend who informed me I needed to get to the hospital right away, but also a few of their neighbors, who heard the screams and one witness who saw Bird drag her back inside the house. He did it, he did it!" Emily pleaded with the staff in tears.

The staff knew the blows didn't come from a fall, as Bird stated. Just then two officers walked in. One walks towards Bird, while the other one stood on the side of him.

"Omar Mize, you are under arrest for the severe beating of Ms. Valerie Taylor. *"You have the right to remain silent. Anything you say can and will be used against you in a court of law. You have the right to an attorney. If you cannot afford an attorney, one will be provided for you. Do you understand the rights I have just read to you? With these rights in mind, do you wish to speak to me?*," the officer continued. Emily stood by Val's side. She tried her best to speak, but the words wouldn't come out. Nothing, but tears.

"It's okay, Val. Let him go. It's time for healing," she whispered.

As the officer arrested Bird and handcuffed him. He looks at Val. "Baby I'll be out soon to take care of you. Only you and I know what happened. A black man in America, don't stand a chance!" he said giving Emily an evil look.

As soon as they led him out the room, there was some relief. The doctor looked at Val and Emily, as the nurse tried to stabilize her blood pressure and her vitals.

"I'm going to encourage you to get some help after you are out the woods. You are going to need another surgery, therapy and a good support system, maybe a domestic violence group. You took a lot of blows and I knew instantly it wasn't from a fall. My mother died from the hands of her abuser and I refuse to see this happen to you, my dear. You almost died. You need to protect yourself at all cost and make sure he is put away for a long time."

Doctor Walker squeezed her hands and then proceeded to walk out the room.

The nurse acknowledged Val and Emily. "I'm so glad her friend, Tyra called the station and hospital and informed us on the events that occurred earlier."

Val figured out that's how Emily knew she was at the hospital. She tried to put the pieces back together from what happened earlier and remember Tyra briefly. Her head started to hurt. Val was getting agitated.

WHO IS HE TO YOU?

Emily knew Tyra and Val's involvement would only end in tragedy. Tyra didn't know anyone else close to Val besides her. Emily tried reaching out to Val's sister by phone and social media but didn't receive a response. Her heart ached for her friend, and she desperately wanted her to get the help she needed.

"Emily, may we use you as a contact for Ms. Taylor? We have no relatives listed," the nurse asked.

"Yes, you may. I'll be here if you need me."

"Thank you, I'll let the others know. She's going to need a lot of therapy."

Emily took a seat as the nurse was leaving out. She pulled out her phone and began to text Marc to fill him in on what was going on. While doing so, she heard a noise only to look up and find Tyra standing near the door.

"I'm sorry, but I needed to see Val," Tyra said, removing her shades revealing a black eye.

CHAPTER SEVENTEEN

V al was fighting and wrestling with herself after she went up against Bird and filed charges against him for almost costing her, her life.

At the local women's shelter where she ended up, she expected to accomplish a lot in her thirty-day stay, like attend therapy, counseling, meet with a lawyer, secure employment or social assistance, and find permanent housing. Val was trying to gain her strength back and gain the confidence she lost in order to feel whole again. She noticed so many other women at the shelter and some with children battling the same issues, some worse than others. Val wanted to stay to herself because she was too afraid to get close or open up to anyone. Val knew Bird would find out about her whereabouts and send someone for her, just because she pressed charges against him.

Val snapped out her thoughts, looking up to find a woman standing in front of her. "Hello, my name is Sabrina," she said extending her hand.

WHO IS HE TO YOU?

Val stared at the woman before greeting her back.

"I'm Valerie, but you can call me Val. Is there something I can do for you?"

"Nah, I just noticed you staying to yourself and wanted to come over and introduce myself. I haven't talked to anyone since I been here. My therapist thought it was a good idea to meet other women, since we are all here with similar issues."

"Oh I see. I'm not interested in making any friends. I just want to get my life back together."

Just like that, Sabrina walked off and headed towards another area of the room. Val felt bad, but she just wasn't in the mood for small talk or dealing with people. Her face looked distorted, hair was all over the place and she felt like shit. She was barely moving around good. She sat up in her chair with a bandage over her nose and then pulled the picture out her pocket of her and Bird, of happier times. Val stared at the picture touching Bird's face. "Oh how I miss you."

She knew in her heart; they were destined to be. They were young, so in love with one another, yet she couldn't understand how they got to a painful place in their lives. Deep in her feelings, she was startled.

"Is that him? Your abuser?" Sabrina hands Val a water bottle, looking over at the picture in her hand.

"It's none of your business! Can I help you?" Val asked, getting agitated.

Sabrina, instead, pulled up a chair and sat in front of Val. Val was starting to get pissed.

"I actually acted the same way you are, when I first got here. Didn't want to be bothered, looked at every photo of my abuser, shut people out and so on, all while I was hurting in the inside. It's a part of the healing process," she added. Sabrina then pulled up her shirt and pointed to a hole she had in her side. "This isn't love, although I thought it was. I was beat, burnt, and shot, all while I thought it was love, by the one man that said he'll never put his hands on me."

Val dropped the picture and put her hand over her mouth in disbelief. "He did that to you?"

"There's more. But compared to you, it looks like you got off easy. That nose will heal. My holes are scars for life. I wasn't as lucky, but I'm alive."

"So is he still out there? My God!" Val asked as Sabrina showed her the other holes drilled into her skin and scars she endured.

"As of today, he's dead. The detectives notified me that he was found dead in a back alley with three gun shots to the head. I identified the body this morning when they notified me with a picture of his deceased body."

"He got what he deserves! Karma is a bitch!"

"And yours will get what he deserves as well. Now I can live in peace and not fear, but honestly, I loved that man with everything in me and probably wouldn't have left until my life depended on it."

Sabrina picked up the photo off the floor and tore it in pieces tossing the scraps in the trash. "I don't think you need that anymore. You are brave and beautiful, that man means you no good."

Val was speechless and didn't bother saying anything about the photo. Sabrina was right, yet Val was afraid of starting over without Bird. She knew she was safe at the shelter, but most importantly, she needed to heal so she could not be afraid anymore. Val watched a lady with her daughter and it brought tears to her eyes, to know she was almost in the same position with a baby prior to the miscarriage. The little girl looked to be at least two years old and the mother was bruised and battered. Val wanted to go over and reach out so bad, but something kept holding her back. She couldn't bring herself to get up and walk over to the lady, who seemed to be having a hard time caring for the girl with a broken arm. She noticed Sabrina headed over offering to retrieve the child, so she could have a break.

Sabrina consoled the little girl and then looked over in Val's direction. Val took a deep breath and closed her eyes and did the one thing she hasn't done in a very long time and that was to pray.

"God my Father, thank You that I have the assurance that You will never leave me nor forsake me. Forgive me for the times when I've failed and disappointed You. Amen."

Val pushed herself out the chair and started walking. Her body was still in so much pain, that she almost sat back down. She knew she couldn't hide forever, so she needed to make use of her time, and be a blessing. Those women just may end up being her backbone.

CHAPTER EIGHTEEN

TWO YEARS LATER...

Val reminisced; a lot had changed for her in a few years. She sat thinking, today was the anniversary date of her leaving the women's shelter, scared and afraid on what was ahead for her. Val moved all the way to Austell, Georgia to get away from the city and to start over. It was a little ways from her family, who she doesn't talk to, but next door to her best friend, Sabrina. The two became very close after their time ended at the shelter. Val is also close to some of the other women she met there as well.

Val stayed in a one bedroom condo and couldn't be happier. She could come and go as she pleased, and not have to worry about anyone except herself. She bought most of her furniture and house needs at the Goodwill and from yard sales. When she left the shelter, she found out she only had a thousand dollars in her bank account after all those years of saving and contributing to her and Bird's bank account. Where that money went, she didn't know. She had to make do with what she had and make it work. She vowed not to ever put herself in that situation again. Emily helped her seek employment with a firm in her area, taking a pay cut, but it was income coming in and a start until she landed back on her feet.

Val made a cup of coffee, a bowl of brown sugar oatmeal and sat on her patio. That September breeze was refreshing. She couldn't remember a time in her past when she sat down and enjoyed her own company without feeling guilty. Upon leaving the shelter, she vowed to leave her past behind her. She hadn't spoken to Tyra at all and often wondered how she was doing. She received several emails from Chanel, but never responded. Her therapist thought that was also a part of her past and not her problem. She wanted to reach out so bad, to tell her it was okay to come out of hiding, since Bird was put away, but left well enough alone.

"Hey, you, what do you have planned today?" Sabrina asked stepping out of her patio in her gown, peeping over.

"Good morning. Looks like you had a rough night."

"You can say it was a good one. Lance came over last night and we stayed up 'til the wee hours of the morning."

WHO IS HE TO YOU?

"At least somebody is getting some, heffa!" Val said as they both laughed. "I'm going to head down to the supermarket in a few to pick up some things, and maybe to the Goodwill and head back because I need to write up a proposal for work."

"You and that damn Goodwill!" Sabrina stated, laughing. "I'm just kidding, shid your place looks nice! You are good with refurbishing things and making it look new. If you're up for it later, maybe we can go have a drink and get out for a minute."

"Sounds good. Maybe I'll find someone to bring home."

They both laughed. Sabrina turned back to walk in her condo as Val looked at her phone. She opened up her Facebook and looked at her mother's pictures from a fake Facebook page she created. She hadn't talked to her mom and sister in a long time. Val was really frustrated that the ones she loved the most turned their back on her, not even giving a damn that she was in the hospital. No one cared. She sent her mom a direct message with her number to call her and to let her know she needed her in her life.

Val went inside and put her dishes in the dishwasher, then put on some clothes to head out. She wanted to beat the crowd and thought about catching a movie, while she was out.

Her phone rang as soon as she got down the street. She didn't recognize the number but answered the call anyway. "Hello."

No one said anything on the other end, but she heard static. "Hello," Val said again.

"Hi, sweetheart. Are you okay?" a woman spoke on the other end.

"Mom? Is this you?" Val asked, turning into the supermarket and slamming on her breaks.

"Yes, dear, this is your mother."

"Oh mom, it's so good to hear your voice. I missed you so much. How have you been?"

"I've been doing pretty well. My diabetes is getting the best of me, but I've been constantly praying for you. I'm so glad to hear that Bird is in jail."

"Mom he's been locked up almost two years now. I'm doing alright, couldn't be happier."

WHO IS HE TO YOU?

"Two years? Why am I just now hearing from you?" Thelma asked confused.

"I thought you knew. I tried reaching out to you and Shai a few times and never received a response. My friend, Emily tried reaching out as well and I thought no one wanted to have anything to do with me."

"Valerie Renee Taylor, I'm sorry I thought it was the other way around. I didn't know you tried reaching out, I just so happened to go on Facebook and saw your message come through. You know your sister also has access to my Facebook as I barely know how to work that thing. She never told me you've been trying to get in touch with me and I ask her all the time if she's heard from you. I didn't know if you were alive or not. I've been sick worrying about you."

Tears started rolling down Val's face; she knew Shai was behind all of this. She was always trying to control their mom and her thoughts, especially while she was with Bird. "I'm sorry mom; I can't believe Shai would do this, as I almost lost my life and had no relatives in site. So much has happened, and my evil sister is just that; pure evil!"

"It's okay, sweetheart. God has answered my prayers, I knew I would hear that voice one day. I miss you so much. Please come see me soon, so I can see that pretty face."

"Mom I'll be there to see you tomorrow, please don't tell Shai I'm coming over. I would love to see her face."

"I can't wait to see you, so I can curse her ass out! All this time, I thought that man of yours didn't want you to see me," she said and Val could tell she was just as happy as she was. "I love you so much and can't wait to see you. The address is still the same."

"Love you mom," Val said and hung up.

She sat in the parking lot and cried tears of joy. All this time passed and her mom never got her messages. She wanted to cook her something special to take over when she went to visit her. That damn Shai was in for a rude awakening. She got some nerve. She hated her so bad, that she tried to cut Val out of her mom's life. *What a trifling bitch of a sister*, Val thought.

WHO IS HE TO YOU?

Val went into the supermarket for a few things but ended up with a buggy full of groceries. She had some coupons stored and hoped not to go over her budget. She was very frugal when it came to things, so that she could have every penny and get back the life she once had as far as her finances goes. She loved the smell of fresh fruit and organic items.

She picked up fresh salmon, so she could make her favorite dish. She could live off of salmon and fish alone. Val was in a better place mentally and physically, she just needed to find her a good church home. She usually buys things to make and take down to the shelter as often as she could.

"Excuse me, you dropped something," she pointed out to the gentleman looking at the selection of wine the store carried.

He retrieved the paper that fell from his hand. "Thank you. There is a reason I made this list," he said turning to her.

She stared at him, with her mouth wide open. The gentleman turned his head and started to walk away.

"Bret Smith?" Val called out.

He turned around trying to figure her out, "Yes, do I know you?"

"Bret, it's me Val. You are a long way from Charlotte, what are you doing all the way over here, especially this side of town?"

"Valerie Taylor? I'm sorry I didn't recognize you. You look totally different. Girl come over here and give me a hug," he said, making her feel some type of way.

She reached out and gave him a hug and a huge smile. "Yeah I had a little work done. I broke my nose and a few other issues, so I had to get some things fixed. Do I look that bad?"

"Val you have never looked bad. You are and will always be a beautiful lady. I just didn't recognize the Valerie I know. Sorry about that," he said without making her feel so bad. "I actually moved back to Georgia about a year and a half ago. I have my restaurant Ventana's and another business here and said why not. I'm actually heading over to a friend's house for a bar-b-cue. I was in the store to grab some wine to take over. Last time I saw you, you were at your mom's birthday party at my restaurant. I asked your sister about you and she said you guys haven't been in communication. Are you married yet?"

WHO IS HE TO YOU?

Val's head started to spin at that moment between her trifling sister and her past, her anxiety was getting the best of her. But she smiled, "That is awesome. I'm sure your family is glad to have you back in town and no I'm not married, that relationship wasn't right for me and as for me and Shai I don't know if we'll ever see eye to eye. You know how she can be."

"Question is, what are you doing on this side of town? Thought you were a city girl, residing in a big mansion," he said laughing.

Val didn't see shit funny but gave a smile anyway. "I actually stay over by this way. I have a condo, not a mansion. After my relationship, I wanted something smaller and to be in a different area, away from everybody, and so far so good," she responded, by telling him what he needed to know. It wasn't his business how she lived.

"I totally understand. Well you still look good and still owe me a lunch outing, remember? I still have that email, you promised."

They both laughed. "I'm not surprised, you still have that email. It was good seeing you, but I have to run," she quickly stated, rushing towards the register, because her heart was racing and she felt her anxiety kicking in. Her medication was in her car. Val put her items on the conveyor along with her coupons. Little did she know, Bret was standing behind her. She was about to panic. The cashier rung up her items and then proceeded with scanning her coupons.

"Ma'am did you get the Cranberry juice, the coupon is not going through?"

"No, I'm sorry you can hand it back. Please hurry," Val said.

"Please add this wine, I'll be paying for her items as well," Bret mentioned to the cashier.

"No, Bret you don't have to do this, I got it."

"No, I don't, but I want to. We go way back, let me take care of it."

"The total is $97.88; will you be paying by cash or card?" the cashier asked.

Bret proceeded to use his card, as Val stood in the background trying to hurry and get out of there. She didn't want him to see her that way. She also had to learn how to relax and not worry about what people thought about her, something her therapist always pointed out.

WHO IS HE TO YOU?

He handed her the receipt.

"Thank you, so much. You didn't have to do that, you know."

He walked her out to her car, helped her put her groceries into her Honda Accord and dropped the buggy off, only to come back.

"You have anything planned like now? I would love for you to tag along to the bar-b-cue with me, if you're up for it."

"I'm not sure if that is a good idea. We just met up and besides I look a mess."

"Girl we go way back as I said in the store. I have seen you at your best and your worse. It doesn't have to be a date, just good ole friends hanging out. You don't know these people, so you'll be good."

"I appreciate it, I'm just..."

"Just what?"

Val was really scared to let him know where she lived but have known Bret most of her life. She knew he wasn't Bird but was fearful for some reason.

"Can I meet you in about an hour or so and we go from there?"

"I get it, you don't want me to know where you live. I understand and if that is a yes, we can meet up in a few. I can go drop off the items and meet you at the park-and-ride, if you prefer."

"Thank you for understanding. Let's exchange numbers and give me about an hour to take the groceries home and get bar-b-cue ready."

"Sounds good."

They exchanged numbers and got in their cars. Val took a Xanax once inside her car. She really needed to get out and was kind of glad to run into Bret but wasn't ready to jump into anything or invite him into her entire world.

She hurried home to change and didn't notice Sabrina's car. She needed to let her know where she was, as they always did. Val was a nervous wreck, as she wanted to go, but didn't feel like being bothered. She hated looking at herself in the mirror, as it reminded her of Bird and all he caused her. The surgeries and her face. She could see how Bret didn't recognize her; she had another person's face attached to her body.

WHO IS HE TO YOU?

She had to shake it off, before she started to feel sorry for herself and not think about it. It always put her in a deep depression. She just recently started getting out, as she was afraid of the stares, like people knew what she went through. Val tried burying herself inside her home, only coming out for work. Between her therapist and Sabrina, she was slowly coming around.

"Val get it together," she told herself. "Don't let your past control your future." She got dressed and texted Bret. She was ready.

CHAPTER NINETEEN

V al was a nervous wreck, but she was enjoying Bret's company at the cookout. Bret had only known Jamie for a few months, but it seemed like longer the way they carried on. Jamie had this one point five million dollar home and wanted to throw a big bar-b-cue for his wife's birthday.

"Hey, man. Who is this beautiful young thing you have on your arm?" Jamie asked Bret, with his beer and wife in tow.

Val smiled, looking around, then at Bret who looked at her trying to figure out what to say.

"This is Valerie, she's an old friend I'm trying to pursue," he said laughing as well as Jamie and his wife.

Jamie looked like he was maybe in his late forties, in good shape, Val could tell. He was black as hell, with a nice salt and pepper beard and clean fade. He was admirable.

WHO IS HE TO YOU?

"Hi there, I'm Stacy, Jamie's other half," his wife stated, extending her hand out to Val. "Bret is a nice man, please enjoy the pursuing," Stacy said jokingly.

They all laughed. Val was a little uneasy at Bret's statement. Hell she was just going with the flow. *What did he mean by pursue,* she wondered.

Stacy had long hair, which was nicely done, with a natural look about herself, but wasn't too flashy. She was very pretty. Val could tell she stayed up to date with the latest trends, in her Gucci attire. From her head band, Gucci flip flops, shirt and skirt to match.

"We will get back with you and let you two enjoy the cookout. I'm so glad you came. We have every alcohol you want to drink and food you want to eat. My chef also has a seafood broil and I know how you like seafood, Bret."

"Jamie, you trying to get me to stay the night I see."

"Brotha, we got room!" Jamie replied as him and Stacy walked off greeting other visitors.

Val followed Bret to the open bar. "What would you like? If I can recall a margarita, perhaps peach?" he asked her, smiling.

"You got it!"

Jamie was right, they had everything you would want to drink behind that bar. The atmosphere and weather was perfect. Val was glad she went home to change and fix herself up, she didn't feel too out of place.

Bret carried the drinks to an open table and proceeded to the server line. He grabbed two plates; Val could see. He came back with all the fixings. Hot dogs, ribs, chicken, pulled pork, snow crabs, shrimp, baked beans, coleslaw, you name it, he piled it on the plates.

"Who's going to eat all of that? I don't eat that much."

"Good, then it's headed in a to-go plate, for later," he responded laughing. "Girl you better eat, it's too much food not to enjoy and free."

Val ate what she could and was quiet in the process. She didn't know what to say to Bret, they just reconnected a few hours ago. It was awkward.

WHO IS HE TO YOU?

"So what did you mean by pursuing me?" Val bluntly asked, sipping her margarita, which was perfectly made.

He almost choked, not expecting her to ask. He licked his fingers from all the barbecue sauce on the ribs.

"Us meeting up like this after all this time. We are both single and it's only right for me to want to heavily pursue you now. Our last encounter, your dude wasn't too happy and took you out your mom's party. I knew he wasn't right for you then. Now is our time, if you just sit back and go with the flow," Bret said, honestly.

"Wow, and okay." *That was a lot,* she thought to herself. "Right now, I'm at a place to just focus on me. I lost myself in my last relationship and it didn't end so well."

"Please stop right there. I'm not asking you to do anything different at all. Let me pursue you and you just go with the flow. I'm not ole dude, and I want you to know who you are. What does Val want? I've known you for some time now on a friend level, but always thought of you as so much more," he said to her, making eye contact. "Boy wait until I tell yo' mama you came out with me to a cookout; she's going to have a fit."

Val giggled because her mom thought highly of Bret. It just never happened for them. Val needed to hear those words from Bret in order to move forward. She was going to relax more and enjoy the moment. She had nothing to lose; besides she hadn't been out with a man in a very long time. She and Sabrina go out often, but it's different with a man. Val didn't think, Bret was her type, but neither was Bird and that went left.

Bret finished what he could on his plate and wiped his hands.

"I would like to toast."

"What are we toasting to?"

"To us. A new start, friendship and just going with the flow."

Val was skeptical at first, not sure of Bret's intentions, but wasn't going to ruin the moment. They picked up their glasses and made a toast. She finished her drink and needed another one. "May I?"

Bret took her glass to refill her margarita. Val felt a cool breeze as the sun was going down and enjoyed the music and scenery. There were people playing cards, dancing, and mingling all around. She was kind of glad she ran into Bret and got out the house. It was so much better than going to the movies. Bret came back to the table with their drinks and a slice of pecan pie, which was her favorite.

"Just one slice?" she asked.

"As I remember, pecan pie is your favorite. Besides, I think I've had enough for tonight," he chuckled.

Once Val finished with her pie, they mingled around for a while, as he introduced her to a few people in the restaurant business. One of the gentlemen invited them to his Cafe for some Jazz. Val was beginning to feel overwhelmed but kept smiling. Bret made sure she was included in all the conversations and laughter and didn't leave her side.

"I guess we should be going. I didn't mean to keep you out for so long. I told my manager I would be by the restaurant this evening."

"I'm ready when you are," Val replied, as she was ready to go and be in her own company.

They said their goodbyes and left. The ride back to her car was relaxing. Bret talked briefly as his phone rang, most of the time it had to do with the restaurant.

She actually liked how he handled business but could see how much that could come between any relationship.

"I'm so sorry. I had to handle those calls; I didn't get a chance to handle earlier. I appreciate you tagging along with me, as it was good to see you earlier and reconnect. I hope this won't be the last time I see you."

"I'll leave that up to you. Remember, you are doing the pursuing," Val said with a wink.

"Alright now. I'll be calling you tomorrow, then," he said as they both laughed.

"I had a really good time; it was much needed."

They arrived at Val's car, as Bret got out and opened her door. "Please call or text me to let me know you got home. If I don't hear from you in the next thirty minutes, I'm calling you."

Val smiled and gave Bret a hug. He waited until she drove off first, to proceed. She felt pretty good at how her day went. It was the first of many to push forward, as her therapist would say.

WHO IS HE TO YOU?

As soon as Val arrived at her mom's house, she was scared to get out of the car because if Bret didn't recognize her, surely her mom wasn't going to either. She took a deep breath and proceeded to get out the car. She grabbed the sweet potato pies she made her mother earlier that morning because that was her favorite pie.

She was also glad to see there were no other cars in the yard but did call first to make sure before she drove over. Standing at the door waiting for her to open it seemed to take forever. She was anxious to see her mother.

"Is that you, my sweet Val?" she asked unlocking the door.

"Yes, mama it's me," Val replied.

Thelma got the door open and looked stunned. "Baby what happened to your face?" she asked looking around as if someone may be with Val.

"Mom it's a long story, but it's me. Please can I come in? These pies are getting heavy," Val said as her mom made her feel uneasy about her looks.

Val looked around the house, noticing new furniture and lots of pictures. Val held up one of what she used to look like and quickly put it back down. She sat the pies on the table, then turned around with Thelma on her heels and gave her a big hug.

"I'm so glad to see you. I missed you so much. It's been a long few years without you in it."

"Sweetheart I've been praying for you every day. Everyone has been asking about you and I had no way of getting in touch with you. Your phone number seemed to have changed. Please let's sit, so you can tell me about this new face. You know God don't like it when we go to changing our appearances. He made us all a certain way, you know," Thelma said. She took Val's hand and rubbed it, as if something was troubling her.

"Mom my face isn't that bad. But I had surgery, as you can tell. I have some metal plates and screws in to repair a broken cheekbone. I also had to have Rhinoplasty surgery to realign and fix my nose, and teeth implants in the front," she continued as she opened her mouth for her mom, "Basically a face lift, a little color lightening and also a damaged kidney that's still healing, all resulting from the abuse I took from Bird."

Thelma jumped up out the seat, "Say what? That man did that to you? I mean baby I knew he was controlling, and y'all may have fought, but not like this," she said putting her hands over her mouth. "Oh sweetheart, I'm so sorry, you could have died!" She added, as tears strolled down her face. "That mother..."

Val continued confiding in her mom how Bird stood over her and beat her with a bat, while kicking her, as well as her shelter experience and now that he's in jail, she's in a much better place. She had to stop and catch her breath as telling that ordeal made her relive it all over again.

"Sweetheart I totally get it now. I'm sorry if I made you uneasy by staring at you, but you are alive and you're still is pretty as ever. I'll take that face any day," Thelma said, reaching out to give Val a big squeeze. "That bastard is going to get his! You know, sometimes it takes an overwhelming breakdown to have an undeniable breakthrough. I just wished I could have been there for you."

"It's okay mom. This moment is everything. All we can do is move forward."

Just then, the door opened and Val jumped because she didn't want to be seen, nor asked any questions. She knew she would eventually but wasn't ready to face her entire family just yet.

"Mom, where you at?"

Val knew that voice. Shai walked in looking like a bag of money. She had on fake Chanel from head to toe. Val knew she kept her out of sight because she was taking their mom's money. It was always about her.

"Do I know you?" Shai asked Val, looking at Thelma.

Val stood up not ready to face her sister nor she pleased with her. She stepped closer, as Shai made a frown. "Val, is that you under all that makeup?"

"Thought you could get rid of me?" Val replied.

"Girls, let's have a seat and talk," Thelma intervened.

"What did you do to your face? Oh, let me guess Bird didn't like your old face, so he gave you a new one?" she said.

Before Val knew it, her hand was across Shai's face. Her sister was already treading on thin ice, and her comment made it worse.

"Val please stop it, Shai zip your damn mouth and don't say another word!" Thelma hollered. "Now sit your ass down!" she demanded.

WHO IS HE TO YOU?

Everyone took a seat, "Val, I'll deal with you later. Mom I need twenty dollars until tomorrow," Shai asked.

Val rolled her eyes in disbelief. She knew Shai was robbing their mother blind. "Girl I don't have any more money. You just took my last yesterday!"

"So where that nigga at? Val you been MIA catering to him, so you mean to tell me he let you out the house?" Shai said, as she kept poking.

"Mom I'm about to leave before I catch a case and end up like Bird, I don't have time for Shai and her remarks. I will call you this evening."

"Wait, Bird's in jail?"

"Shai please. You really need to apologize to the both of us for hiding Val's messages, and changing our numbers so she's not able to get in touch. You told me she had the number. You've been lying this whole time!"

"Don't go blaming this on me! Her man kept her away, like how he dragged her up out your birthday party!" Shai yelled trying to back up her claim.

Val grabbed her things and kissed her mom goodbye. She was just so glad to feel her touch. She knew arguing with Shai was pointless and telling her about her ordeal, just for her to rub it in her face. She had a new outlook on life and it didn't require going backwards.

"I sure can't wait to dig into these pies of yours. You know I love sweet potato," Thelma spoke. "I'll talk to you later and don't worry about your sister. I'll talk to her and fill her in, so she won't make another nasty remark."

"I love you, mom."

Thelma rubbed her face, "I love you, too. You are still pretty, remember that. God got you."

Val smiled and then hissed her way out the door. She noticed a guy on the front porch smoking a cigarette and knew he belonged to Shai, looking all dusty. She got in her car and headed back home.

It was still early, so she had time to Netflix and chill with herself before starting a new week. Val ignored Bret's text messages for that reason as he popped up at a crazy time in her life. The bar-b-cue was cool, but Val wasn't interested in dating, she was still trying to get used to looking at herself in the mirror. Bret was a nice guy, but not her type.

Val needed to talk to Sabrina because moving forward seemed to be easy for her. Val would feel good for a moment, and then go back into a slump. Just as her thoughts started to consume her, Bret called and she decided to pick up.

"Hello beautiful. I was hoping you weren't dodging me. I pray your day is going well," he greeted and spoke.

"Sorry, I didn't respond. I was visiting mom."

"I see, my future mother-in-law," he laughed.

Val smiled. "I made and took her some sweet potato pies. Those are her favorite."

"I didn't know you could cook. I see I may have some competition," he joked. "I was calling because I would like to see if you're available this evening, for maybe dinner or coffee?"

"Bret, I don't know. I'm really tired and want to be alone this evening. It's nothing against you. I just need some me time, if that makes sense," Val replied, not feeling guilty.

"I totally understand. Maybe we can get together for lunch or something one day this week, perhaps?"

"Sure. I can fit you into my schedule," Val giggled.

"How about this, let me order you some take out and have it delivered, if you don't mind me having your address, so you can just go home and prop your feet up. I won't take no for an answer."

Val was not ready to give out her address, but knew Bret wasn't a threat. "What the hell, that sounds good."

Val didn't feel like cooking nor did she have the extra funds to eat out like she wanted. She was going to welcome the blessings. Whatever they may be.

CHAPTER TWENTY

A trip to the grocery store turned into so much more for Bret. He and Val have been seeing each other pretty regularly for the last few months and he was enjoying it. Val was finally coming out her shell and loosening up. He had a business trip coming up soon and wanted to see if she would like to tag along.

Val told Bret a little about her and Bird's relationship over dinner and he couldn't wrap his mind around how someone could be verbally and mentally abusive to the woman he loved. She had all the qualities a man could ask for, including no kids, which is great for him because he doesn't have any of his own, although he came close, but the child ended up not being his, which dissolved that relationship.

Bret knew how Val loved grilled food and was finishing up, so dinner could be ready when she arrived. He had a few sides from the restaurant sent over to go along with the meat he was serving. He didn't know why he had butterflies in his stomach but it was something special about Val and now that he had a chance with her, he didn't want to mess it up. He grooved to Keith Sweat in the background, as he took out the Stella Rosa wine in the fridge he had chilled.

Moments later, the doorbell rang. He quickly washed his hands and ran to the door.

"Hey sunshine! You look really nice," he said as he took a moment to admire Val's beauty when he opened the door.

"Well, thank you! You don't look bad yourself," she replied.

"What are you doing with that wine?"

She pulled out the bottle in the bag, "Sir, this time we getting lit! This is the watermelon Cîroc! Oh we drinking tonight!"

"Oh that's on a whole other level," he laughed. "What we celebrating?"

"Just figured I'd mix it up. We had so much fun at Emily's last weekend and that Cîroc punch she mixed was on point. I haven't had that much fun, since, well I can't remember."

WHO IS HE TO YOU?

Val and Bret were invited to Emily's for her birthday gathering. She also brought Sabrina and Lance along and it was an epic night. She got a chance to reconnect and chat with Marc and Derrick. Marc was really happy to see Val in a good space. No one judged her or her new look, as far as she knew.

"Girl you know that ain't punch?" he said shaking his head.

"Yeah, I know. What smells so good?"

"All your favorites! Salmon, shrimp, ribs, pork chops, and ribeye steaks."

"Can I help with anything?"

"Just make yourself a home."

Val opened the Cîroc and poured some in two cups. She went behind Bret and washed the dishes he had in the sink, while filling him in on her outing with her mother and Sabrina. Bret didn't know what had gotten into Val but she was in a talkative mood and he liked that she was really opening up to him. He really like Val and her company. He was hesitant about asking her to go to Chicago with him but felt like he had nothing to lose. She could use a few days stress free and he could too.

Bret knew, Val had been through a lot in her last relationship, a reason he didn't really push the envelope on what really happened to her face. He wanted her to tell him what happened, when she was ready. Bret's last relationship was also heartbreaking, built on lies, and deceit. He was destined to fine true love, eventually.

The food was finally ready, as he prepared two plates. "I really had a great time at Emily's. It was nice to meet your friends."

"Thank you for tagging along. It felt good to not be the only one without a date," Val replied as she laughed. She helped Bret transfer the plates to the table, as they sat. Val's cup was almost empty as she proceeded to pour more alcohol.

Bret watched as Val continued to drink. He didn't want her to drink too much, but for her to feel comfortable around him.

Bret cleared his throat, as they both said their grace and dug in their food. "I have an upcoming trip to Chicago for business and was wondering if you'd like to accompany me there," Bret quickly got out. "We could stay a few extra days and do some sightseeing. Chicago is really nice."

Val cut her eyes at Bret as if he asked her to jump off a cliff. "Chicago? I have work and can't afford to take time off; you know that."

"Val, if you're worried about finances, please don't. I got you. Take a few days off. We both need a vacation," he pleaded.

He watched as she was hesitant to speak. She was thinking. He just wanted her to say yes.

"Let me know the dates and I'll see what I can do."

"So, does that mean, yes?"

She winked her eyes and continued with her food. Bret knew she wouldn't let him down, he was going to make sure she was on that plane. Val just needed someone to make sure everything would be alright. If he had to pay her bills, then that's what it was. He just wanted to cater to her and show her the world, something he always wanted in a relationship. His last relationship was based off material things and an outside baby by his ex and not enough love.

"So, what's on your mind?" he asked, curious.

"Oh nothing. Who would have thought we would be here after all this time? I really like it."

Bret couldn't believe what he was hearing. He didn't think Val was really interested in him like that but was glad to know she liked what they were doing. He didn't want to pressure her too much, just enough to let her know he wanted to build something with her.

Val paused and continued, "I mean over the past few years, I was with someone who didn't see my worth and I put his own happiness before my own and honestly, I thought that was love. The time I was in the women's shelter, taught me how to be strong and get to the place I am in now."

"Wait a minute, you were in a women's shelter?" Bret asked, trying to understand what Val was telling him. "I'm sorry, I didn't know. What really happened, if you don't mind me asking?"

"No, you're good. I trust you. I just have a hard time talking about it or him. Bird, my ex-fiancé, was abusive verbally and physically as I've told you. I dealt with it for many years. The last incident could have killed me, which caused me to have my nose altered, screws in my cheekbones, and a facelift, among other things, so I look at things differently now," Val continued looking Bret in the eyes. She was embarrassed because deep down, she knew Bret thought she had it all together, but this was her life. "I'm sorry, Bret I just want you to know, that I appreciate you, but also wanted you to know why I fall back at times."

Bret took his napkin, threw it on the table and ran to Val's side. He had never seen her so vulnerable and was glad she shared that part about her past with him. He held her in his arms and didn't want to let go. He could never put his hand on a woman, not even his ex when he found out the baby wasn't his. He caressed her face, "Val you are still beautiful to me, regardless of what happened. I want you to know, I am here for you and promise not to ever hurt you."

She lifted her head and kissed him softly. That was the most passionate kiss she'd had in a very long time. "I'm sorry," she whispered.

"There is nothing to be sorry about. You needed to get that off your chest. May I ask, where is Bird?"

"In Valdosta State Prison, serving a ten-year sentence. I am notified of his every move."

"I don't trust that prison crap, often times notifying people falls through the cracks. I'm going to buy you a gun. He'll never come near you again!" he added.

Val and Sabrina did go to the shooting range often, but never could get the nerve to purchase a gun. Deep down, she knew, Bird wouldn't be an issue once he got out. She appreciated Bret's concern about her safety.

They both finished up their meals and headed to the living room to binge watch *Top Boy* on Netflix. Bret poured Val a glass of wine as well as himself and had a slice of cheesecake.

"I can't eat another bit," Val said.

"Me either, but it looks good," he replied laughing.

Bret turned on the movie and noticed twenty-minutes into it, Val was asleep. He put a blanket over her and paused the television to watch her sleep. He couldn't believe the woman he's always dreamt of was sitting next to him, sleeping. He laid his head back as he was getting restless himself. Just as he closed his eyes, Val uttered something.

"Hey, why did you pause the show?"

WHO IS HE TO YOU?

He opened his eyes to Val, "Well I didn't want to watch it alone. You drifted off."

"I'm so sorry. It was all that good food you prepared."

"Blame it on the food," he said smiling.

He sat up, gazing at her and her natural beauty she held. He couldn't help but wonder, "What if we..."

"We what?" Val asked, not letting Bret complete his question. She pulled herself up and scooted closer to Bret. She didn't hesitate yet kissed him so passionately her knees buckled.

Bret's manhood sprouted as Val's hand moved down to his shaft. He was surprised at Val's sudden move. He definitely wanted to make love to her, but when she was ready. Bret kissed Val on her neck as she made her way inside his pants, stroking his dick. This time, Bret's knees buckled. He wasn't expecting her to come on so strong.

"Val, what are you doing?"

"Whatever you want to do. Are you gay?" she blurted.

He laughed as it became awkward. "No, babe. I just want to make sure you are ready for the next step, that's all."

"Oh, I'm so sorry." She grinned. "I am," she replied moving her hand to caress his chest.

He stood up and picked her up, carrying her to the bedroom, where he positioned her on his king size sleigh bed. He then went around the room to light some candles and turned on some soft music that played in the background. Val laid on the bed, as she started undressing herself, not waiting on Bret. Her body was trembling in anticipation. Bret moved in and stood over her, admiring her naked body. He hasn't seen a woman that beautiful in a very long time.

"You are so damn beautiful," he said, as he remained standing, grabbing her toes from the edge of the bed, inserting them in his mouth one by one. He was so glad she had nice feet because he had a foot fetish and that was the first thing he noticed about her or any woman. He sucked them gently and made love to her feet like they were the last thing on earth. He knelt before her at the edge of the bed, slowly planting kisses at her leg. He kissed and caressed her inner thighs, causing her to breathe heavily. He couldn't wait to taste her sweetness but wanted to make sure he kissed every part of her body first.

WHO IS HE TO YOU?

Val caressed his head as she felt his breath near her clitoris. Bret made his way to heaven's gate and thought he saw Jesus, but instead it was the pinkness of Val's vagina. He needed her. The special moment had presented itself at last, finally. Bret lifted Val's ass, so he can make love to her so deeply. His tongue was a weapon as he slowly sucked her juices, skillfully, not leaving a drip to drop. Her wetness flowed like puddles. Val chanted Bret's name as she wanted more. He felt her body shiver as he made his way to her ass and back to her pussy and repeated the process. His hands crept up to her breasts as he toiled with her nipples, as they hardened with thrill due to his magical touch. His thickness was becoming too much to bare. He pause locking eyes with her, as he saw his desire for her. Val reached in for him, as Bret leaned in and kissed Val with intensity. His hardness pressed and pulsated against Val's belly, as she was getting delirious with heat and longed for him to be inside of her. She thrust her hips to manifest what she wanted and Bret replied as he entered her warm and wet vagina gradually. Their eyes met, due to the tightness of her walls. He continued as she encouraged him by raising her hips and rocking with his rhythm. Their bodies were in perfect harmony, a match made in heaven. Jazz played softly in the background, making the mood more romantic. Bret made sure to please Val with so much passion, without limits as she deserved, but really wanted to fuck her so bad. His smooth strokes made Val call his name with so much affection. At last, they were one in the most intimate way, as lovers.

Val was tender, but everything to him at that moment. Her past didn't matter; she was delicious, graceful, and rare. Bret took both of them to paradise, through a wave of ecstasy. Val tried to speak but couldn't manage getting out her words. Her legs contracted uncontrollably, letting Bret know he was fulfilling her needs.

"Sweetheart, are you okay?" He whispered softly in her ear.

"I'm more than okay, I am superb," she replied back in the softest voice. "I can't control myself, I'm about to cum," she added.

"I was waiting on you before I climaxed," he added.

Val repeated Bret's name over and over, until she reached her peak. His deep voice was stuttering, as he climaxed with depth. His body stiffened, as sweat drenched and he became breathless. He rolled over on his back, pulling Val's body close to his chest. He leaned in and kissed her on her forehead. She closed her eyes as she rested in his arms. Fatigue and sexual gratification pulled the two into a peaceful coma. The dream of making love to Val was a real delightful experience they both enjoyed.

It was after midnight when Bret awakened lusting for Val like a dog in heat. They had already made love several more times before falling asleep. Their bodies connected, never finishing the flick they were trying to binge watch, however, they ended up on his king size bed making love, then the shower. He knew Val was exhausted and probably even sore, but he just couldn't get enough of her. She mentioned it had been years since she'd last been with a man. She was definitely making up for it.

He watched her as she slept, wanting to wake her. Bret's hand slid up and down her warm naked body, yet she didn't budge. He knew she needed the rest after all the hard work she put in pleasing him. Bret's eyes rolled back as he flashbacked of Val riding him backwards cowgirl style and it was mind blowing. Her back faced forward as her warm pussy slid up and down his dick, exposing her nicely shaped apple bottom. Her muscles contracted perfectly on his shaft, making him bust back to back. The connection they both shared was very well matched. Bret silently beat himself for being selfish, but he was feening for her love, her touch, that magical pussy. She was like a drug; he had got hooked on overnight.

Val's phone started ringing and he jumped. His heart pounded. *Who could be calling her after midnight? Was there something she wasn't telling him? Who could it be?* She moaned as she tried to wake up, but she was out of it. The phone stopped, only to ring again. Bret sprouted up from the bed, to go across the bed to grab her phone, so he could put it on vibrate, but noticed it was Sabrina calling. He really hesitated on answering it, but figured she was checking in on her.

"Val, wake up," he whispered, as he gently shook her, trying to wake her. Sabrina phoned again. "Sweetheart, Sabrina is calling, would you like for me to answer?" he asked, as he shook her again. He decided to answer, not sure if that was a yes or no.

"Val, are you okay?" Sabrina asked on the other end of the phone, before he could say anything.

"Hi, Sabrina, this is Bret. Val is currently sleeping. I tried waking her, but she hasn't budged, but she is in good hands," he stated, looking over at Val as she squealed trying to wake up.

WHO IS HE TO YOU?

"Thank you, Jesus! I was worried. I haven't heard from her and I didn't see her car. I guess you must have given her some good dick, or else, her ass would be at home by now!"

"I think Val will speak to you now," he quickly stated, uncomfortable responding to her comment. "Babe, its Sabrina," he passed the phone to Val as she sat up.

Val took the phone from Bret, "Sabrina, I'm sorry I forgot to check in. I'm staying over at Bret's tonight. It's too late to be driving home."

"I guess good dick will do that to you," Sabrina giggled on the other end of the phone. "I'm glad you finally got some, it's been awhile for that cobweb."

"Girl, I'm about to hang up this damn phone on you," Val laughed. She felt good to finally get some. "We'll talk later, I'm about to attend to my man, now," Val said, not realizing what she just said.

"Your man?" Sabrina questioned. "Okay, I hear you girl. Go attend to your man, then."

Val was speechless. She glanced over to Bret, She didn't know what she was feeling after the evening they had. They have been spending a lot of time together and she has grown to really like him. He looked her in her eyes, "Tell me what's on your mind and heart because I like the idea of being your man," he winked.

Bret would love to hear those words coming out of her mouth. Val was incredible to him and the total package. He was completely everything that a woman dreamed of. He knew she desired to be loved, correctly, just as he did. He wanted nothing more than to make her happy.

"Talk to me, what's on your mind?"

"These few months, have been everything to me. You've showed me so much in the short time we've been hanging out and the fact that you put my needs first really scares me. Tonight, really assured me that you could be the one, that is, if you would want to be my man," she blurted out. Val looked at Bret's facial expression, which beamed with a huge smile.

"Hell yeah! I am your man, so is this official?" he asked being funny and laughing.

"Yes, if you want to put a title on it. I'm your girl and you're my man!" she said, not holding back.

WHO IS HE TO YOU?

Bret leaned in and kissed her. He pulled her close to him and gave her a deep long kiss. "Thank you, for making me happy," he said.

"And thank you, for bringing life back into my life."

They both seemed to be on cloud nine. He wanted nothing more, but to make love to her all night long. They both longed for love and found it in each other.

CHAPTER TWENTY-ONE

"Girl, you know how I said I wasn't into him like that? Well, I'm into Bret for the long haul," Val replied with a smile. "I mean this is not the type of love I'm used to. The brother was everything! Kind of like how I envisioned Larenz Tate with me in Love Jones," she added, tickled at her own response.

Sabrina walked over to Val, with her robe on. A pair of Victoria Secret slippers and bonnet on, with her coffee mug in tow. "Did you say, love?"

Val could not hide her facial expression. Her words were just flowing freely and she couldn't seem to keep them intact. "Yes, I think I'm in love with Bret. There I said it!"

"Wow!"

Val leaned against the counter. She was scared out of her mind. *What if Bird got out of jail and found her, harming Bret? What if he broke her heart? What if everything she was feeling is just a dream*? She longed for the right love, that she really felt safe and secure with. Bret made sure she was his priority.

"Val you deserve happiness. We both do, given what we've been through. I think Lance came along at the right time in my life because I thought I would be single forever. Who wants a shot up woman? I have bullet holes in my body, but he accepts me for me and so does Bret," Sabrina reassured her friend. "Val, I love you like my sister. He's the one. Stop doubting yourself and the what ifs. Love is a beautiful thing."

Indeed it was, Val thought. Bret was like a good friend to her, now her lover. She looked forward to his calls, instant messages, and spontaneous adventures. She couldn't wait to accompany him to Chicago. Val was trying not to be afraid but couldn't help but feel that way. Her life was always built around Bird and Bird only.

"Well we made it official last night that we are a couple. Girl, I got a man!"

Sabrina was all smiles. "The ladies at the shelter will be thrilled to hear you say those words."

"I know. I'm taking food there later, please come. Also I'd like you to come back for brunch, my sister is bringing my mom over. I'd like you to meet them."

"Girl, listening to you talk about your sister, I need to go pray. You guys have a lot of unresolved issues you need to iron out."

Sabrina was right. She was more than a sister to her, than Shai has been over the years. She wanted her mom to see that she was really okay and doing well on her own. Thelma was really concerned for Val and offered to move in with her, but Val needed her own space. It was good for her. And now that her and Bret are a couple, who knows what the future holds? She couldn't wait to tell her mom that Bret was the special guy in her life.

"I'll be back soon. I need to go lie back down, for a few hours."

Soon as Sabrina left, with Val's coffee mug in hand as she usually does, she cleaned up the kitchen. She was going to have a light brunch she was putting together. She was already missing Bret. He was never her type, but he grew on her. She was finally in a happy place and wanted to help the other women in the shelter get there. She knew how hard it was starting over and adjusting all over again without the one person you thought would be there. Val sat at the table to check her emails and finish her coffee, and then her phone rang. The name that came across now reads *babe.*

"Good morning, babe. I miss you." Val could tell Bret was smiling from ear to ear on the other end of the phone.

"I miss you more. You sound kind of sexy. Anybody over there?"

"No, silly," she smiled. "You need to be here, though."

"I'm coming soon. Don't temp me to come sooner," he said. "I know your mom and sister will be coming by in a few hours. I will have one of the assistants at the restaurant, bring over some food. I don't want you lifting a finger."

Val's eyes grew big. "Babe, I bought all this food. You don't have to do that; mom loves my omelets."

"Omelets are also on the menu. I want you to be well rested for our trip tomorrow. I want you to try to relax and let me take care of you because I enjoy it," he stated.

Val smiled. She didn't know what she did to deserve someone like him. He always catered to her needs and it was very sexy to her.

"I really appreciate that. You really are God sent. I can't wait to see you," she beamed, as she blushed through the phone. "Just maybe, I will do that thing you like later."

"Baby now you talking! I'm getting a hard on just thinking about you. Honestly you complete me," he added. "Surely we met at that store for a reason. I am falling head over heels for you."

"And the feeling is mutual. I love you."

"You what?"

"Nothing, I said the feeling was mutual."

"No, you said you love me. Do you?" he asked her as he heard her the first time. Please don't hold back from me because what you're feeling, I desire that same love as well."

Val's eyes bulged but she was afraid to repeat what she stated. She didn't want to be the first to say I love you, but she did. She had nothing to hide or loose, she thought. "Bret, I love you, There I said it."

WHO IS HE TO YOU?

"Valerie Taylor, I love you more," he replied. They both were in love and needed to hear those words. Tears filled her eyes. Happiness was finally paying her a visit. She owes it all to God, because she could have been dead or stuck in an abusive relationship with no way out. *I love you* replayed in her head over and over. She just so happened to glance at her email while on the phone and noticed an email from Chanel. It was the strangest thing since she hasn't spoken to her in a very long time. She wanted to be done with any and everything that reminded her of Bird.

"Babe, I have to go and get ready so I can prepare for the food when it arrives. I can't wait to see you," she hurried and rushed him off the phone.

"I'll be over as soon as I finish some loose ends at the restaurant and I'll stay over tonight, so we can head to the airport in the morning."

"Sounds good. Love you." Val stated and hung up.

She opened Chanel's email.

Hi Val, please let me know if everything is okay. You haven't returned any of my previous emails and I noticed Bird's profile online, as I was researching his whereabouts. I am thinking about coming back to

Georgia, to visit my family and so everyone can see how big Tyler has gotten. I've attached his picture below. Isn't he handsome? I hope and pray life is finally treating you well, I would love to know you are okay though and bring Tyler to meet you, besides you have helped us out tremendously.

Chanel Gaulty

Val looked at Tyler's pictures and saw all of Bird's features. He was a nice looking teenager. He had Chanel's eyes and lips. She hoped that he didn't grow up to resent his father. She wanted so desperately to respond, but thought that leaving well enough alone, was the best remedy. She didn't want to create a hostile environment for her new life because she had a good heart. She helped Chanel out with Tyler in the past because that was the best thing to do at the time. It would be good for Chanel to stop running and go visit Bird, that way it would do them both some good. Val read the email again and decided to close her laptop. She wasn't in a position to help everybody; she was still getting herself together.

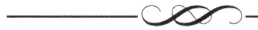

WHO IS HE TO YOU?

"As soon as Sabrina gets here, we'll go ahead and eat," Val stated. Sabrina was just jumping in the shower when Val phoned her.

Thelma was looking around Val's condo, while Shai was glued to her phone. It was a little awkward. Val went ahead and started preparing the mimosas and figured she would break the awkwardness. Shai hadn't once looked up since she'd gotten to Val's place. She wished she would have sent a car to pick up her mom instead, but Thelma insisted her and Shai needed to talk.

"Sweetheart, I'm so proud of you. Your place is really nice. I still can't believe you moved way out here."

"Thanks, mom. It's really not that bad. I like the area."

"I'm just worried that you are all alone, out this way," she replied. "Once I meet this new man of yours, it might give me some assurance."

Val noticed Shai glanced up after Thelma's comment. She was curious to know as well but scanned her head back towards her phone.

"You'll meet him soon and I know for a fact you will be very pleased."

Shai couldn't take it anymore; she stood and walked towards the kitchen. "So is it someone we know?" she asked.

Just as she was about to respond, Sabrina walked in. She had on a neon jumpsuit, hair in a bun, and her slippers. Her face was of natural beauty, she didn't need any makeup, but she revealed a tiny scar on her face from her abuser.

"Hello, everyone. I'm Sabrina," she announced. She noticed Shai and then Thelma. "I live next door, so I usually just let myself in," she cackled.

"Finally we can eat," Shai blurted, not being friendly. She stood in the background and surveyed Sabrina.

Val started handing everyone mimosas and started setting the table with silverware. She gazed over at her mom talking to Sabrina. They were snickering about a picture Thelma was holding. Val wanted to break the discomfort with her sister, since she was still in the kitchen, holding her glass ready to eat.

WHO IS HE TO YOU?

"So how have you been, sister?" Val conceded, almost spilling her drink.

"Actually, I've been pretty good. Started a new job last week, and still trying to take mom to her doctor's appointments. You know, her diabetes is getting bad."

"Well congratulations on your new job and no I didn't know about mom's diabetes. Maybe I can assist on getting her to her appointments," Val offered, not sure what Shai was getting at. She was the one that cut her mom out her life, but she wanted a peaceful afternoon and refused to figure out what she needed her to do. Shai always threw jabs and Val wasn't buying into it.

Shai took a sip of her drink, frowning up at watching their mom chuckling with Sabrina on the couch.

"That would help, if you can assist. Anyway, I wanted to really apologize from the last time I saw you, about saying some awful things about your face, I'm sorry. Mom filled me in and I'm glad that bastard is locked away. I also apologize for my actions with mom," Shai confessed. "I was upset when you put that bastard first and left mom's party all because of him. I figured we didn't matter, but I understand when someone is being abused, so is there mind."

"It's more than that sweetheart," Sabrina added, walking towards the kitchen. "Your sister and I bonded in the shelter and I don't regret that. I didn't listen to my family either, yet here I stand with several gunshot wounds, but I'm grateful to be alive," she continued, showing her sister her scars.

Thelma's mouth was wide open in shock as well as Shai's. Her glass tumbled as she caught it. She moved in closer looking at Sabrina's wounds. She was totally in shock. "Oh my God!" Thelma shouted.

Val moved in closer to hug her sister. Thelma smiled with relief. They all sat at the table, surrounded by pancakes, sausage, salmon benedict, bacon, omelets, scrambled eggs, ham, grits, shrimp, biscuits, chicken, and waffles. There was plenty of food and plenty to take home. She was glad to see Shai talking to Sabrina and not making it awkward. They both were glued in listening to Sabrina talk about her experience in the shelter and how she got there. It all made sense to her mom and sister, regarding her life. The food was delicious as usual. Bret sure did come through for brunch, he went all out.

WHO IS HE TO YOU?

"Now Val, I know you didn't cook all of this, where did this food come from?" Shai asked.

"Ventana's, their brunch is off the chain!" she said in excitement.

"Oh, the place we had mom's party?"

"Yes, that's it."

Shai started looking sideways, trying to figure out how this food got all the way on the other side of town. She didn't respond back. There was silence as everyone dug in and ate. Val got up to retrieve her phone, just in case Bret phoned her, and then noticed two text messages from him.

"Everything okay?" Thelma inquired.

"Yes, mother," she responded. "How is the food?"

"The food is delicious, but your omelets are amazing."

"I told Bret you would say that," Val stated.

"Bret?" Thelma and Shai asked in unison.

The doorbell rang and she knew it was Bret, as he was just in time. Val got up and rushed to get the door, not responding. He texted and stated he was on his way, a while ago. Everyone looked to see who it could be. Just as she opened the door, Bret kisses her on the lips.

"This is the man in my life," she presented to her mom and Shai.

Thelma smiled and stood up, slamming her napkin on the table. Shai remained seated sipping her mimosa. Thelma reached in and gave Bret a hug, "Oh wow, this is awesome," she concluded.

"Thank you, mom," he chuckled. "Hi, Shai, it's good to see you again."

"Hello, Bret, good to see you as well. Take care of my sister, now," she warned. "I knew something was up, when she stated the food came from Ventana's. That's a drive out here."

"I promise to take real good care of your sister," he added, kissing Val again.

Thelma smiled as she approved. Val fixed Bret a plate as he headed into the living room to watch football. Once Val sat back down, she couldn't take another bite of her food, as she was stuffed. Val was glad her family had the opportunity to visit her, because it was important in her progress. She was also glad Sabrina came by and joined them, it made things a little easier.

"Sweetheart, you are starting to look like your old self again," Thelma asserted across the table.

"You think so?"

"You are beautiful regardless. Look, the family has been asking about you. Why don't you and Bret come by the house next weekend and I can fix dinner and invite everyone over."

"Mom, not now. I'm not ready to see everyone at this moment. I don't want to have to answer questions, maybe later," she quickly replied. "Besides, we'll be in Chicago."

Bret brought his plate into the kitchen and inserted himself, "I'm taking my baby to the windy city," he added.

"Just bring me back a souvenir," Thelma teased.

Brunch was a success, Val thought. She made everyone take to-go plates home and cleaned the kitchen. Bret was on the couch sleep, as football was watching him, so Val thought she would join him. She wanted nothing more but to cuddle up with her man, where she finally felt safe. He was everything Val needed and so much more.

CHAPTER TWENTY-TWO

The river and lakefront cruise Bret took her on last night was amazing, Val thought. She and Bret had been in Chicago for a few days and every day it was something different. He had made the trip thus far very memorable. Their suite at the Waldorf Astoria was nothing short of amazing. The spa and steam room was wonderful. She was waiting for Bret to return from his meeting with a team of investors about opening up another restaurant in Chicago. Bret was really excited and if all goes well he planned to open soon.

Val stood on the balcony of the high-rise hotel and admired the view in her Versace dress Bret surprised her with. It was a nice flowing wrap dress, that fit her shapely body perfectly. She pinned up her hair in an updo and applied some makeup to her face. She was beginning to except her face for what it was and love it regardless. Val used to hate to look at herself in the mirror, yet, Bret taught her to embrace her face because she was more than stunning. Just the thought of looking at her face always reminded her of Bird and what he put her through. Well, as her therapist says, *what she allowed.*

She poured herself a glass of wine and then opened her laptop. Val wanted to check her emails from work to make sure nothing important was lingering. She ended up Skyping Sabrina while she was working to check in. Sabrina was so glad to hear from Val; she was already asking for souvenirs. Val was head over heels for Bret. He had always flirted with her in the past, but Val couldn't see straight as long as she was with Bird. She ended up on her Gmail account and stumbled across another email from Chanel. This time, she started to respond. Val typed, deleted, then typed again not sure what she was doing, but she wanted to let Chanel know she was okay. She began to let her know it was time to stop running and noted where Bird was doing his time, if she wanted to go visit with their son. It was time for healing and to move on. *What could Bird possibly do in jail?* Val didn't usually make the best decisions but thought responding to Chanel was the least she could do. She immediately heard the doors open and quickly signed off and closed her laptop. She stood up, almost spilling her glass to embrace Bret.

"Baby, the meeting went well. I know for sure Chicago will be a great location for Ventana's. The investors were impressed with my business plan," he said beaming with excitement. Bret was all smiles as he loosened his tie. He was on cloud nine.

"So, when will you know something?"

Just then, Bret's phone rung and he immediately answered.

"Yes, sir, you got a deal!" was all he heard from the caller.

"Please send the documents over to my email. I'll look them over and get them back to you as soon as possible, partner!" he replied, smiling from ear to ear. Bret quickly hung up the phone. "Yes, baby we did it! This will be awesome for us, I got big plans!"

"Congratulations, babe, but you did it. I'm so happy for you," she declared. "And what do you mean, awesome for us?" she asked curious.

Bret had to stop and gather his composure. He was overly excited. "It's clear I want to be with you, I'm just including you in my plans, that's all, but I have been thinking. I'd like you to consider the idea of us living together soon. I mean you can move in with me, or I can buy a bigger condo or house in your area. I just hate going home and leaving you alone at night, I want to see you every day," he mentioned.

"I'm not sure if I'm ready for that right now, maybe later. You have to understand, that starting over and being alone financially was the best thing that could have happened to me. I love you, but let's just give it a little more time." Val was just putting the pieces to her life back together; she didn't want to have to depend on another man for happiness. She was learning to love herself all over again. It was good to have someone who adored her, but she was also trying to heal. "Listen baby, It's not you. I just need time to think about it."

Bret caressed her face with so much sensitivity and pulled her close. "Woman don't take too long thinking. I could wake up to this beautiful face every day." He planted a kiss on her forehead.

He released her and went to grabbed something out of his jacket. It was a small Pandora box, he handed it to Val. "For you."

Puzzled, she didn't ask any questions, she just opened the box and noticed a gold pendant shaped heart on a gold rope. She opened the pendant and then covered her mouth, "Baby this is so cute." A picture of them together at Jamie's cookout, their very first outing. The inscription read, 'Love Saw It.' She was speechless, as she was getting teary eyed.

"Turn around," he said.

She did as she was told and let Bret put the necklace on her. She touched the pendant as that was the nicest thing, someone had ever done for her. "I'm so grateful, and lucky," she expressed.

"I just want to take care of you, as you deserve and make you happy at the same time, Valerie," he smiled. "By the way, that dress looks damn good on you!"

She laughed as she started flaunting her weight around modeling the black and gold Versace dress with slits on the side. He slapped her ass as she walked by, shaking his head.

"Alright now, I got time!"

"And, so do I. You already know what you do to me. Let's get out of here to go celebrate and I'll let you put it on me tonight," he winked.

She touched his dick and he was rock hard. She then glanced up at him and winked back. "Grateful that is all mine."

He shook as his soul almost left his body from her touch.

Val had been going back and forth with Sabrina over text messages regarding her thirty-fifth birthday party. Val didn't care for Jazz, but Sabrina loved it. Since it was her birthday, Val promised to be there. Lance was out of town, so she was bugging Val while she was still in Chicago.

When Bret started licking her clitoris, she threw her phone on the floor. He didn't mind giving her oral sex. He did it so well it brought tears to her eyes. Val closed her eyes and took a deep breath, as she gyrated her hips. The warmness of his mouth was incredible. He lifted Val's ass up and proceeded to pull her close to him. He planted kisses around her belly button and between her thighs.

"Here, I was about to feed you grapes," she moaned.

"Is that so? I know exactly what to do with those grapes!"

WHO IS HE TO YOU?

He popped a grape in his mouth and went back down to the edge of the bed. He spread her legs apart on the silk sheets and inserted the smashed grape inside her pussy and then began slowly sucking it out of her. It was intoxicating. He repeated the process a few times. His tongue covered her vagina in ecstasy. Val was out of her mind; she felt her soul leaving her body. She spread her legs apart even wider; giving him more access to have his way with her. She moaned in agony. He inserted two fingers in her wetness, pleasing her the way she needed. He slowly eased his way on top of her, making contact with her lips. As they kissed passionately, his finger slid out of her juices, and then he entered her gently in slow motion. He released his lips, just so he could sit up and watch his manhood slide in and out of her. Val couldn't help but watch as well, kind of like watching porn. She wanted nothing more than him to fuck her from the back.

Bret sped up the pace, as sweat dripped off his forehead. His body shifted giving her a full ride. He wanted all of her.

"Oh, Val..." he whispered. "Baby, I love you."

She felt him trembling as his adrenaline was coming and his knees started to buckle. Val's body was spiraling out of control from Bret's lovemaking. The intensity was greater and she too was about to reach her peak.

Bret's body jerked, as he pulled out of Val, letting the tip of his fluids drip out and onto Val's stomach. Her vagina was still pulsating and then her body started to shake as well in the highest form of climax. Their bodies were a match made in heaven. Val had never enjoyed sex the way she did with Bret.

He simultaneously went into the bathroom and retrieved a warm washcloth and then came back to the bedroom and wiped Val down like a newborn baby, as well as himself. He slid right under her, so he could cradle her in his arms. She laid her head on his hairy chest and heard his heartbeat. His body was warm, amazing, and full of satisfying gratification. She was very well pleased.

CHAPTER TWENTY-THREE

C hicago was nice, but Val was so glad to be back home in her bed. She and Bret had an awesome time and she was considering moving in with him. She wasn't one hundred percent sure, but she was sure of his love for her. They had the opportunity to discuss their growing relationship and her being a partner in his business. Everything seemed to be moving a little too fast for her, but her mom and Sabrina assured her it was a good thing.

Val thought about some of the ladies at the shelter and knew they too could have a good life, given their circumstances. When she looked back over her life, she wasn't sure why God put her in that situation with Bird, but she could appreciate it now. It made her look at things differently and value Bret more.

She was standing in the mirror touching up her makeup. She couldn't wait to celebrate with Sabrina at her birthday party at the Velvet Note. Val wore a nude jumpsuit that hugged her body in all the right places, with matching nude heels. For an evening of jazz, she thought she was nicely dressed for the occasion.

Val heard the door unlock and quickly jumped. The smallest things gave her anxiety.

"Babe, I'm here," Bret called out.

Val wasn't sure if giving Bret a key to her place was a good idea, but she got tired of getting up to unlock the door when he came over to stay the night after leaving the restaurant and besides, she has a key to his place.

"I'm in the bedroom, sweetheart."

Bret crept up behind Val as she touched up her hair and kissed her on the neck. His hands then slid to her backside.

"Alright, now! You want to make it to this party or not?"

"Not really. I can sit here and enjoy the night with you," Bret replied, smiling. "You smell really good."

"It's Burberry."

WHO IS HE TO YOU?

Bret moved back and took a seat on the bed. He admired Val standing in the mirror. She was beginning to love herself. Val grabbed her Louis Vuitton pochette and was ready to go. Her phone rung and it was Sabrina.

"Sweetheart let's go; Sabrina is calling. I told her I was on my way a while ago," Val started as she laughed.

"Oh, Lord, she's going to be blowing you up."

Val turned out the lights as Bret locked the door behind them. She stood at the car door and patiently waited for Bret. He didn't want Val to ever touch the car door to let herself in, if he was around.

Bret's champagne Infiniti QX80 smelled like new money. The interior was sophisticated, with saddle brown leather featuring all luxury features that Val was scared to touch.

"Babe, you know I love all genres of music, but jazz is my favorite," he pointed out.

"That's good to know because the way you try to sing, Maxwell and Kem, I thought you were an R&B fanatic, but then again you try to rap Drake," she theorized.

They both giggled. She rested her hand on his knee, as he drove to the venue.

"Bitch, it's about time you got here!" Sabrina said.

"Bitch, this is Atlanta. We ran into some traffic!" Val admitted. "Anyway, the decorations came together beautifully and you look amazing, I must add."

"You know, I came to slay!" Sabrina chuckled.

Val scanned the area for Bret and noticed he was talking with Lance. Sabrina had a few other friends and couples there Val didn't know. Sabrina introduced everyone as people arrived.

"I invited Shai. She called me on the way over here and mentioned she was called into work."

"I'm glad she called you because she usually doesn't. I know she was picking up some extra shifts," Val stated. "I left your gift at the house, in a rush," she proclaimed.

WHO IS HE TO YOU?

"Girlfriend, you didn't have to get me a gift. Your friendship is enough."

Val squeezed her hand and smiled. Bret walks up and stands next to her. As the party got on the way people were mingling and dancing. There were other party goers in the building, Sabrina just had an area sectioned off. The Velvet Note was an upscale Lounge that featured a nice ambiance, American cuisine, nice art and live jazz. They also played dance music at a certain time to get the crowd going. People were eating, they were taking pictures, and drinking.

Val heard, *She's a Bad Mama Jama* come over the loudspeaker and knew, Sabrina requested that song.

"Come on, y'all," Sabrina ordered everyone.

We all went to the dance floor and got in a soul train line. Bret was standing on the side, recording and taking pictures. He laughed at Val, because she almost busted her ass. Then *Da Butt* song came on and the crowd went wild. Val and Sabrina sung along to the music.

That's right!

Shake your butt

Come on!

Gimme that butt!

Gimme that butt!

Sabrina got a big ol' butt (Oh yeah)

Val got a big ol' butt (Oh yeah)

Sheri got a big ol' butt (Oh yeah)

Yvette got a big ol' butt (Big ol' butt)

And Trina got a big ol' butt (Oh yeah)

Janielle got a big ol' butt (Oh yeah)

Ol' Nicole got a bubble butt (Oh yeah)

Little Keisha got a big ol' butt (Big ol' butt)

Gimme the butt!

After building up a sweat, they left the dance floor area, as the DJ was preparing for the live jazz band. Val cuddled next to Bret, who rubbed her shoulders. "You looked stiff out there on that dance floor," he joked.

WHO IS HE TO YOU?

"Ha, ha, somebody got jokes! At least I got out there, sucker!" she hissed. "You better be glad, I love you."

Bret cackled, "And I love you more."

The lights started to dim. The atmosphere was soft yet laid back. Jazz was never Val's forte, but being with Bret made everything she disliked in the past worth loving. Val looked over at her friend as their eyes locked and winked at her. They were finally in a happy place of their lives and she couldn't be happier. She was glad to have a friend like Sabrina. They have been depending on each other since their time at and out the shelter. So celebrating her birthday with the love of her life, meant a lot to her.

The band was playing, while Bret hissed in her ear. He made her want to take every inch of clothes she had on off, right there in front of everyone. She giggled like a schoolgirl and then, rested her hand on his knee. Val glanced over at the other couples and they were all enjoying the entertainment. Val has never felt as safe before in her life as she did at that moment.

"Sweetheart, are you okay?" he whispered.

"Yes. Are you having a good time?" she replied.

"Of course. Spending time with you is always a good time. I'll have an even better time, when I get you to the house and you can do that little dance I like," he teased.

Val blushed. He was very sensual. She thought she hit the jackpot when they reconnected. It took a while before Val let down her wall she had held up for so long in fear of her past. She glanced around the room and made eye contact with a gentleman who looked like darkness to her past, and then anxiety came over her. Val rubbed her eyes, then glanced again and realized she wasn't seeing things. The man, who turned her life upside down, was now gawking at her. Bird sat on the opposite side of the room scouting. "This can't be happening," she mumbled to herself. He was with a woman who favored Val in every way possible. Her posture, even the way she used to wear her hair, resembled her.

Val's body started to shift and she became tense. She turned her head, and then the images started to reappear of her looking at herself in the mirror after having reconstructive surgery. Her face was finally healed from the brutal attack, but she could never forget her skin hanging from the blows, teeth missing, broken nose, she was a mess. Bird was a woman beater and he almost cost her, her life. Val's family disowned her, at least that's what she was led to believe because of her constant running back and forth to him, every time he put his hands on her.

"Babe, I'll be back. I'm going to the ladies room," she announced.

"Don't have me waiting too long, or I'm coming to get you."

Val stood from her chair, trying to catch her balance. She only drank two glasses of wine but felt tipsy. She walked to the back of the lounge, went into the ladies room and stood in the mirror trying to catch her breath. Her heart was pounding, anxiety started to creep in, yet she was trying to calm herself down before going back out. She didn't have her anxiety medication on her and felt like she was going to lose it. Val felt like running out of the club, leaving everyone behind, even Bret. She didn't want to ruin her makeup by splashing water on her face, so she gathered herself together. Val exited the ladies room only to bump into the man who was not supposed to have any contact with her, whatsoever. Val tried going around him, but he grabbed her by her arm and pulled her to the side. She became fearful once again, but afraid to scream. The thought of him beating her with a bat, came to her mind at that moment.

"Who is that nigga you with?" he asked, forcefully. "Didn't I tell you I would kill you, if I ever saw you with another nigga?" he threatened, with full force. "You didn't think I would recognize that new face of yours?"

Val jumped, afraid to answer. She didn't want Bret involved in any of Bird's fiascos. She knew Bird and if anything, Bret would be an easy target. Bird looked like he has put on a few pounds, very muscular, now sporting a bald head.

"Val, who is he? You didn't think I would ever get out of jail?" he asked, growling, rubbing her face he once disfigured.

"A friend," she replied, as her voice trembled. "Bird, please leave. I am much stronger now and you are not to be near me," she jerked. "That lady you're with, must be your next punching bag?"

He wanted to punch her, as he balled up his fist. Val knew he hadn't changed a bit. A group of ladies passed by in the hallway, before he grabbed her arm again. Bird looked pitiful, but only wanted to torment her.

"Sweetheart, what's going on?" Bret walked up from behind and asked Val. "Is this negro bothering you?" he asked, noticing Bird's hand on her arm. She watched Bird's facial expression towards Bret and was fearful of what was to come.

"I'm just checking out my ole lady, partner," Bird proclaimed. "Who the hell are you?"

"Val, who is he to you?" Bret asked demanding an answer.

Val was shaking. She didn't want to say anything, but knew she had to. "This is my past. Remember me telling you about my last relationship and how it almost cost me my life? This is Bird."

The lady he was with, emerged and walked up behind Bird looking confused. She looked as though she had a black eye, with a face full of makeup. Yet, Val felt sorry for her because she knew that look. Val looked at her, with tears in her eyes and stepped to her.

"Get out now, before he kills you! I see that bruise under your eye." She touched her face. The lady didn't move, still afraid as Val once was, then she finally jerked away from Val.

Bret took Val by the hand, "Sweetheart, there is no need to be afraid anymore. He is nothing to you," he said turning to assure her everything was going to be alright.

"Nigga, you have no idea who you're dealing with. Val is...."

"Hey, what's going on?" Sabrina asked, walking towards them. "And who is he?" she asked noticing the frown on Bird's face.

"This is Bird."

Sabrina became terrified, trying to figure out what he was doing out of jail and how. "Oh hell no, I'm going to get security!" she yelled and then ran back the other way.

Bird grabbed the woman by the arm, pulling on her, as he tried to walk away in a hurry, while looking back at Val and Bret. "This isn't over, Val." He and the woman jetted towards the front exit.

Val broke out in tears as she trembled in Bret's arm. "Baby, I'm so scared. I didn't know he was out, I really didn't," she cried.

He consoled her, "We will call the warden and find out what's really going on. He won't put his hands on you ever again!" Bret tried his best to calm her down. He now had an idea of what Bird was capable of and he wasn't about to play his little game. Val was too precious to him, to let go.

CHAPTER TWENTY-FOUR

"I can't believe this is happening! This has to be a mistake!" Val shouted. She paced the floor in turmoil. She was hysterical after coming face to face with Bird.

"Sweetheart, I'm sorry. The warden said he sent out several letters to your P.O. Box and your mother's address. Due to his good behavior and medical condition, he was paroled out early."

Val's anxiety started to get the best of her. She couldn't believe he grabbed her the way he did and questioned her about Bret. She knew then he hadn't changed.

"Please, Val have a seat. We are going to figure this thing out together," Sabrina stated.

"You damn right! I can't believe he had the nerve to grab you like he did. I didn't like that shit!" Bret added. "You're getting a gun and moving in with me, that's final!"

Val fell back on the couch with her hand over her head. It was late. Sabrina and Lance were heading out to her place. Bret walked them to the door. She was no longer scared of Bird, but her concern was him coming after Bret. The thought of her moving on did something to Bird and she saw it in his eyes. She took a deep breath; just knowing he's out there. Val wanted to get to the bottom of the letters that were sent out but didn't want to wake her mother that late.

Bret walked back to the couch and flopped next to Val. He put his arm around her gently and squeezed her tight. She snuggled close to him, inhaling his scent, not wanting to leave his grip.

"Baby everything is going to be alright," he whispered.

He kissed her on the forehead, massaging her temple. Val knew she was safe in Bret's arms, but she felt the need to protect him. Just the thought of seeing Bird gave her the thought of filing for a gun permit. She was not going to live in fear anymore and vowed to protect those around her.

The sound of Val's phone made her jump. It was late and she didn't know who it could be. Bret handed Val her phone, noticing a text from Shai. She finally smiled. For once her sister was checking in on her after seeing Bird at the club. She replied, and then dropped the phone on the floor, resting her head in Bret's lap.

Val woke up to the smell of bacon and fresh coffee. She noticed her gown on the edge of the bed but couldn't recall doing anything. She fell back onto the pillow trying to gather her thoughts to recall the night.

"Sweetheart, are you awake?" Bret asked, peeping in the room.

"I am. You are up mighty early."

"It's a little past noon," he chuckled.

"What? You let me sleep that late?"

"You needed it. Besides you looked like sleeping beauty," he said. "I went ahead and made brunch. Please cover that sexy body and meet me in the kitchen."

"Babe, why is my gown on the edge of the bed?"

Bret shook his head. "I tried to help you put on your gown, but you said no and went straight to sleep, so that's how we slept."

Val felt awkward asking him that question but would remember if she had sex or not. She did remember all the craziness with Bird. Val pulled herself together to go brush her teeth, wash her face and to meet Bret at the kitchen table.

Val was in awe when she got to the table and noticed two dozen roses. She stood there speechless, with her hand over her mouth.

"Baby have a seat, let me cater to you."

"Babe you are always catering to me. When did you have time?"

"Will you just have a seat?" he said in laughter. All he wanted to do was bring a smile to Val's face and he did just that. Bret fixed her plate, poured her some mimosa and then handed her a rose from the banquet. She smelled the aroma from the rose and let out a deep sigh.

"A reason, why I love you so much," she replied.

WHO IS HE TO YOU?

He peaked her on the lips and then took a seat next to her. There was less talk, but lots of smacking. Bret watched Val tear into her turkey bacon and French toast, then she caught him looking.

"Damn, am I smacking to much?" she grinned. "You do make some mean French toast."

"No, I'm just glad you enjoy my cooking. Plus your ass is hungry as hell!" he said, jokingly.

"You damn right, after the night I encountered, I'm starving."

Bret leaned in, with all jokes aside. "Baby, about last night. I talked to your sister this morning. She said she did find letters through a pile of your mother's mail, unopened from the jail."

"Wait a minute, that don't even sound right!" Val interrupted. She pushed her plate to the side, as she sat up straight.

"Let me finish," he added. "You know how your mom doesn't open half her mail because of doctors' bills, they were in that pile, according to Shai."

Val raised a brow, as she heard it all before. Her sister kept her mother away from her, now she was putting her life in danger, with Bird. She wasn't sure if this was another one of Shai stints or not, but she was getting to the bottom of it. Shai did some underhanded things and to believe she didn't know about the letters, didn't sit right with Val.

"Sweetheart, I know what you are thinking, but I do know, people change and I really do hope she is telling the truth."

"Sounds like you are unsure, too. Look I know my sister and the hate she had for me. I just hope and pray she is telling the truth," Val stated, as she rubbed her eyes. She was not even hungry anymore. So much was running through her mind, she needed to get a hold of the documents, to make sure Bird doesn't come near her, again.

Bret reached on the side of the chair and pulled out a pistol. "This is for you. I need you to keep this with you at all times. We need to get it registered in your name, but I have another one."

"A gun?" Val shouted. "I mean, I'm not scared and know how to shoot one, but I don't think Bird is coming near me ever again. We just so happened to run into him."

WHO IS HE TO YOU?

"And that's a chance we aren't taking," Bret stood up and announced. "I saw the look in his eyes and the way he was grabbing on you. He hasn't changed and I would hate for something to happen to you."

Bret was right. Val was in fear and scared out of her mind. So many memories, that she tossed and turned and couldn't sleep. Val took the gun and put it in her purse. She knew she couldn't be with Bret 24/7, so she had to protect herself.

That poor girl that was with Bird, looked so young, yet abused, but that wasn't her issue. She noticed all the signs and saw straight through her pain. Val was finally at peace and happy with her life, for the most part, but she still couldn't shake the fact that she still loved Bird deep down inside. Through all the hurt and pain, she still wanted the best for him and that one day, he would be able to love completely without being physical. Her emotions were all over the place and part of her, wanted closure from Bird. For some reason, she wanted to hear him apologize for how he treated her.

Hours later, Val found herself responding to Chanel's email. Chanel and Tyler were coming to town soon, she hasn't been back to Atlanta in years. Val wanted so bad to tell her Bird was out of prison and that she ran into him, but she didn't want to ruin her excitement, as she had already bought her train ticket. She figured she would tell her during her visit. With all the pictures, she was kind of excited to meet the young guy she helped raised, without Bird's knowledge of her and Chanel's relationship.

It was time for Chanel to stop running and regain her freedom back. A lot has happened over the years and they both deserved to be free and happy of Bird's hold on them. Val just wanted Tyler to know his dad, she thinks it will do them both some good and thinks that is the bulk of Bird's problem, not having his son around. Life was short and there was no time to waste. Val reframed from telling Sabrina anything about her communications with Chanel, for fear of her confiding to Bret. Because she cared so much, she couldn't help it. She wanted to leave well enough alone and go on about her life, but having a good heart, just wouldn't let it happen.

Val closed her laptop and picked up her phone. She dialed her mom and then hung up. She immediately dialed her sister's number and the call went straight to voicemail, "Damn!" she said. Bird's image was triggering things in her mind she didn't want to think about. She redialed Shai's number and kept getting her voicemail, "Dammit, Shai, answer the damn phone!" she yelled.

Val was getting agitated. She was hurt and most of all in so much pain. Thinking her only sister would stoop so low and would let the man who brought nothing but pain into her life, do it all over again. Val knelt down on her knees and prayed to God, that wasn't true. *For once, let Shai have a pure heart.*

CHAPTER TWENTY-FIVE

V al had just had lunch with Emily, as she pulled into Whole Foods Market to pick up a few items before heading home. She took Bret up on his offer to quit her job to be his bookkeeper for the restaurant. It was bringing in a substantial amount on a weekly basis. Bret wanted an extra set of eyes and thought it was best with all the Bird drama.

Val finally spoke with Shai who denied ever seeing any letters from the State prison and promised she would never do anything like that. Val wanted to believe her, but still had reservations, given she kept her and Thelma apart. Sabrina thought that Val should cut her some slack given the circumstances. She didn't want to put Shai in a position to do something stupid, since Bird is now a free man. She agreed, since she was trying to build a strong relationship with her family. Val just needed something to shake the feeling of her sister's betrayal.

"Miss are you going to use this buggy?" a gentleman asked.

WHO IS HE TO YOU?

"Oh, I'm sorry, no go ahead," she responded deep in thought.

Val grabbed a cart and proceeded through the store. She wanted a nice kale salad for dinner, maybe some grilled shrimp and chicken. Val picked up a few items including some new probiotics she wanted to try and headed to the checkout line just as Bret texted her to pick up a bottle of Cabernet. She exited the line and grabbed a bottle as well as a bottle of Chardonnay and placed them in her cart. She proceeded to turn around, but then bumped into a gentleman.

"Oh, I'm so sorry," she said looking up.

"No need," he replied.

"Oh, no! Bird?" Val said, startled. She dropped her cart and fell back on a can of peas. "Are you following me?" she asked, but Bird was nowhere in sight, only shoppers looking at her strange. "Wait, where did he go, where did he go, dammit!" she hollered through the store.

"Ma'am calm down, are you okay?" a store clerk asked.

Val looked around but didn't see him. She didn't know if she was losing it or not, but she knew what she saw.

"Why is this happening to me?" she asked.

"Please let me help you up front and you can have a seat and tell me what's going on," the clerk responded.

"Just help me with my cart and to the register, I'll be fine."

The clerk wasn't so sure. He signaled for the cashier to proceed with checking Val out, so he could help her to her car. He was only trying to help. Val felt sweat forming on her forehead and was getting hot. She just wanted to get home. She paid for her items and exited the store. The clerk helped her to her car.

"God bless you," he said and proceeded to head back inside.

"Thank you!" she called out, distracted by the rose left under her windshield wiper. With all the kidnapping and abductions going on across the country, Val got in her car and locked the doors.

WHO IS HE TO YOU?

She looked around the parking lot and began to get paranoid. "Bird, I know it's you! I know it's you!" she whispered. "What do you want?" she asked herself.

Val began to drive off and decided to drive a little longer, in case someone was following her to throw them off. She knew she had to tell Bret. Everything was getting crazier by the day and she couldn't keep it together.

Val wasn't sure if telling Sabrina was such a good idea. She walked around in circles in her living room with her hands on her hips. Val rushed to Sabrina's place as soon as she got home about her seeing Bird and the mysterious rose on her windshield.

"You know you have to tell Bret, right?" she stated. "I mean, this shit could get really crazy, Val."

"I know, I know, but did I really see him? I mean when I turned around he was gone!"

Sabrina walked toward Val looking her dead in her eyes. "Listen to you. You know exactly what you saw. Who in the hell put the mysterious rose on your windshield?" she said, trying to figure out why Val was acting delusional.

"Do you think he's been watching me? I just can't help but wonder."

"Yes, that's what they do when they can't have you. It turns into stalking," Sabrina responded as she lit a cigarette. She only smoked when something heavy was bothering her or if she was stressed out.

Val knew talking about Bird was only bringing up heavy memories for Sabrina. She decided to end the conversation and head back to her place.

"I understand," Val replied. I'm going to head out and wait for Bret to get home. I'm going to get a protection order in place, although he isn't supposed to have any contact with me. I just want to cover myself in case something bad happens."

"And I advise you to do so. Bret gave you a gun for a reason, use it, if you have to. You have to protect yourself, at all cost!" Sabrina side eyed Val.

Val hugged Sabrina and walked towards the door to exit. She still didn't feel at ease. She thought talking to Sabrina would calm her anxiety, it only raised her blood pressure. Now it was round two with Bret once he got home. She wished Bird was rational enough to talk to her and hopefully apologize, so they could have closure and move on. She didn't want to be looking over her shoulders her entire life, just because he had personal issues.

Val got to her condo and started putting up the items she picked up from the store. She poured a glass of wine, to calm her nerves. Once she put up the items, she checked her email. She had two unread emails from Chanel, stating she would be in town sooner. Her mom was sick and she needed to come see her. She was catching a train and wanted to meet at a coffee shop. Val was so hesitant about responding, she was already putting herself on the line thinking about Bird and having closure. With all that has happened, she still had a soft spot for him.

Val read the email over and decided not to respond and think about it, but she felt the need to let her know what was going on. Chanel didn't know Bird was out of jail. All hell would break loose once Bret found out and Val couldn't let her past destroy her future.

CHAPTER TWENTY-SIX

V al had way too much wine because as soon as dinner was over, she was all over Bret. Val's hormones were all over the place. Bret didn't know what had come over her. He found himself fucking the hell out of Val. When they made love, it was sensual, now they were fucking like two jack rabbits, yet it felt so good. Val was simply trying to block the conversation of Bird out of her mind. She wanted to fuck all night if she had too.

"Babe, slow down, I mean you're wearing a brother out," Bret pointed out.

"I'm sorry babe. I've been holding it in all day. I couldn't wait for you to get home," she replied sheepishly.

Bret gazed in her eyes, trying to find the right words to say. He simply kissed her passionately and Val started to melt. The way Bret caressed her was like no other. Being with Bird was no comparison. Bret was truly a gentleman. He was so passionate. But once again, Bird still crossed her mind.

Bret let up and rolled over as Val caressed his hairy chest. She could lie in his arms all day. She let out a deep breath. Bret put his hand on her chin and lifted her up towards him.

"Penny for your thoughts?"

"I'm good, really I'm good. I haven't felt like this in forever," she smiled.

"So nothing happened today?"

Val lifted her head looking at Bret, "No, what about you?"

"Bird? When were you going to tell me you ran into him?" he asked, sitting up in the bed.

Confused, Val was trying to figure out how he knew. She was going to tell him, but just hadn't gotten around to doing so. She didn't want him to think she was keeping things from him.

"How did you know?"

"I ran into Sabrina coming in and she filled me in. She was just concerned, that's all."

"I bet she was," Val replied and rolled her eyes. She couldn't let her tell him first. "Babe I promise I was going to tell you; I was really trying to block it out. He startled me, that's all. When I turned around, he was gone and then there was this mysterious rose on my car."

"He just so happened to know your car? I mean the sudden disappearance and rose. It was him," Bret said looking at Val. "Babe I don't need you keeping anything like this away from me. He has hurt you one too many times. I can't help, if I don't know."

"I'm sorry. I promise I was going to tell you. Guess it wasn't fast enough."

Val got up and put on her robe. She wanted to end the conversation, but knew he was right and Sabrina did what was necessary. She looked back at Bret. "So what's next?"

"I'm paying to break your lease as soon as possible, so you can move immediately. I'm talking about this weekend."

"That's too soon. I mean he's not coming to this house."

WHO IS HE TO YOU?

"We're not taking any chances. People like Bird will stop at nothing to get their prey back. I've been doing some research and this is only the beginning. With me being in his way, it's making it a little harder for him to get to you. Val, let me protect you?" he asked.

"Sure. I have nothing to lose," she said and walked off. Val felt some type of way as if Bret was starting to control her rather than be her confidant. She was starting to lose sight of the situation.

Val jumped in the shower and ran the water until steam filled the room. A warm shower always helped put her mind at ease. She heard Bret come in, so she turned her back. She opened the shower door and was about to hop in. He quickly grabbed Val and pulled her close to him.

"I'm sorry baby, if I said something out of the ordinary. But, I saw the fear in your eyes at Sabrina's party, when Bird grabbed you by the arm. I just want to be there for you."

At that moment, she knew it was real. She knew Bret had her best interest and only wanted to see her safe. Val never had that type of love to know what's genuine or not, but her heart was softening to Bret.

"I know babe. I just had a moment but do understand you have my back and my front."

"You better believe it! So does that mean you're moving in with me?" he asked smiling, showing off the one dimple he owned in his left cheek.

"That's a yes!" Val beamed. Bret had an oversized house and it would be nice to give it her own personal touch.

She couldn't wait to tell her mom and sister. Val was glad she gave her and Bret a chance. She quickly learned the ones that are not your type, are the ones that'll treat you right.

Val just hoped this put an end to the Bird fiasco, so she could move on with her life and never look back.

CHAPTER TWENTY-SEVEN

Moving Day

The day has come and Val was at peace. She felt good about her decision to move in with Bret. She had her mom come over to help her pack up some things and her sister would be over later. She was a little salty with Sabrina for telling Bret about Bird but tried to see the big picture of it all, so she and Sabrina hadn't spoken that much about the situation.

Val came across some old photos in a shoe box of her and Bird and stared at them. They both had to be in their twenties. Val beamed at the pictures and smiled as she remembered the good times. Bird used to call her his Queen and then that soon turned into the word bitch. She tried to understand the change but couldn't justify his actions. She was nothing but good to Bird and he knew that, any other woman wouldn't have put up with what she endured. She worshiped the ground he walked on, because he used to be so good to her. She thought they were in it for the long haul, little did she know, he had another side to him. Val rambled through the box and then came across a necklace with a cross on it, she remembered the day he gave that to her, but he quickly snatched it off her neck when he thought she was talking to another guy, only to be her cousin. It broke and Val never got it fixed. That incident should have been her sign, but it wasn't, she endured more pain than pleasure, thereafter.

"Sweetheart, in order to move on and heal you must get rid of your past and stay away from what broke you," Thelma spoke standing behind Val as she was holding the necklace and glancing at another picture.

"You're right mom. I just came across this box and it brought back so many memories, like I don't know what went wrong between Bird and I. I loved that man, so much, but..."

"But, nothing. I loved your dad once and looked how we ended up? You just wasted a lot of years and went through so much. I tried to intervene, but sometimes God has to step in and do His work. You endured so much over the years and look how you bounced back. You are a strong black woman, stronger than you know."

Val wiped the tears that had started flowing from her face and put the items back in the box. She really needed to close that chapter and truly move on. One minute she's happy, and then she finds herself still caring. She wanted to believe that he has changed since his incarceration but wasn't so sure.

Thelma reached for the box. "Baby let me have that. I'll go discard these items and you finish packing. No need to be going down memory lane with the devil."

They both laughed. Thelma was right. Val continued putting items in boxes and couldn't believe how much stuff she accumulated. God had been nothing but good to her. She didn't think anyone would want her after the multiple surgeries she went through and then, here comes Bret. He will send you someone just to show you, you are appreciated and that someone will love you no matter what.

Val's phone started ringing and it startled her. She looked around for her phone and then heard it under a pillow. She didn't recognize the number, but it kept ringing back to back from the same number.

"Hello."

"Val, this is Chanel. Hope I wasn't bothering you."

"Girl, you scared me. I wasn't expecting to hear from you."

"Yes, I know. I was in the area and wanted to do a quick drop by and let you meet Tyler. I came in earlier than expected. If it's okay with you I can swing by for a quick visit."

Val was so damn scared; she didn't know what to say. *How was she going to tell her mom that she's been in contact with Bird's baby mama?* She was just being nice and meeting Tyler would give her the opportunity to see the little boy she's been supporting through the years.

"Sure, I'll text you the address. I'm actually packing to move, so it would be a good time to visit."

"Great! Once you messaged me the address, we'll come right over."

Val ended the call, texted Chanel the location and she heard Sabrina's voice in the other room.

"I'm here to help, Valerie Taylor!" she yelled.

Val smiled; she couldn't be mad at Sabrina for too long. She was her closest friend and was glad she didn't fold on her. Val came out the room and hugged her. She was glad she had come over to help. Sabrina held up a wine bottle and two wine glasses.

"Oh mom is outback."

"Doing what?" Sabrina inquired.

They both smelled something burning and looked out the window to see where it was coming from. They noticed Thelma throwing items in the fire pit and dumping all the photos of her and Bird.

"Wait, what is she burning? Is that legal around here?" Sabrina questioned.

"Old memories of Bird and I. She said she was going to discard the items, but I didn't know she was going to burn them," she laughed.

"Welp, out with the old, in with the new!"

They both toast and drank up. Stella Rosa was becoming Val and Sabrina's new go to wine. They both had so much in common, that they should have been sisters. Under the circumstances, she was glad they both connected. Val often wondered what her life would be like, if it didn't turn out the way it did.

"Sis, I'm so proud of you. You deserve to be happy and so much more. It doesn't matter how many chapters you have written, starting over is always good. You are going to like this story better; I can see it."

"Awe, thank you. I think I am becoming the real Valerie Taylor. As I sit and think about things, this second chance is simply amazing. You and Lance are doing wonderful and nothing, but blessings for the both of us."

"Well, Lance and I have been looking at houses and talking about marriage. We had a hiccup as I thought I was pregnant, but it turned out to be a false alarm. I'm grateful it was; I'm not ready to be a mother."

"When the time comes, you will be a great mother," Val added.

"Hey, you, I thought I heard another voice in here," Thelma stated, entering the room. "Y'all's asses in here drinking. We ain't never gone get packed up!" she laughed.

"Mom get you a glass and join the party, we actually got more done believe it or not," Val replied.

They both giggled and turned on the radio as they began packing away. Bret had a driver coming over later to transport items to his place and storage, until they figure out what to do with everything. Val's phone rung, several more times but she didn't answer. The number seemed to be blocked and she didn't care if it was Chanel or not. As an hour went by, Val got a lot completed. She texted Bret, who was going to bring food over shortly, she didn't know what she did to deserve such a loving and caring man like him, but she thanked God every day.

Val heard the doorbell, as Sabrina ran to the door. Val stumbled on items, as she tried to exit the room she was in. She spotted Thelma heading towards the front of the house. She then heard Sabrina, at the door talking to a lady, who had to be Chanel.

As Val stood in the background, her heart raced. It was too late to take an anxiety pill as it sped up.

"Wait, the name Chanel sounds familiar. Are you…"

"Yes, Bird's baby mama. I'm here to see Val, she's expecting me," Chanel responded.

Sabrina and Thelma looked at each other confused. They had no clue why she was standing at Val's door.

Val finally emerged from the background, not knowing what to say. "Hey guys, I see you met Chanel. Please come in," Val blurted.

Chanel walks in with this six foot teenager. She knew that was Tyler from the pictures. He had grown and looked like a spitting image of his dad, height and all.

Thelma walked up behind Val, "You must be out your damn mind?" she whispered and turned and walked towards the kitchen.

"Val can I speak with you for a moment?" Sabrina summoned her.

"Please you guys have a seat, give me a moment."

Val followed Sabrina to the bedroom, soon after Thelma entered. "What's this all about? This is not making sense, why is this woman at your doorstep with Bird's son in tow? The son he created, while you two were together!"

She was trying to find the right words to explain the situation as no one knew she's been talking to Chanel off and on. "I actually told Chanel it will be okay to drop by since I was moving. She has been away since her son was two and her mom is sick, so she's in town to see about her. I wanted to see and meet Tyler, after all these years, so finally this is the actual meeting and this chapter of my life will soon be over."

"Oh my God!" Thelma said and stormed out the room. She was highly upset with Val, after she's been outback burning things. She should have been burning sage throughout the house, if she knew what Val was up to! She clearly didn't understand why Val was holding onto something that brought her so much pain.

"Val you can't save everybody. These people are here, you need to do your little meet and greet and hurry before Bret gets here. This situation really doesn't look good."

"Don't you know, I know that? This just happened when she called earlier. Let me handle this, so that I can send them on their way and everything will be all good."

"If you say so!"

Val walked out the room, her emotions were everywhere, not understanding why her heart was so big, when it comes to helping people and especially Chanel, who had a baby by her boyfriend at the time. She didn't know why she didn't close that chapter with her immediately. But, knew it mostly had to do with staying in touch with Tyler.

As Val sat in front of Chanel and Tyler, she was speechless.

"Tyler, this is Valerie. Your dad's ex fiancé and the lady that helped me when I needed things for you," she stated.

He stood up to hug Val and she embraced him.

"You are your father's son, handsome, I may add."

"Thank you. I've heard a lot about you, all good things," he stated. "So you leaving town?" he asked.

"No, I'm actually moving in with my boyfriend. He lives on the other side of Atlanta, and we think it's the best move for the both of us."

"I'm so happy for you. You got out one crazy situation, to be blessed with what God intended for you. Praying my time will come one day," Chanel intervened.

"It will, all in timing, I've learned," Val assured.

Val and Chanel sat going back and forth for about a half an hour. She was glad to learn so much about her and her adventures over the years. She was finally at peace to hopefully stop running, since Tyler was of age. She has missed out on so much over the years, due to hiding from Bird. Tyler would be an upcoming senior and wanted to play basketball, with his height he could get a scholarship into a decent school.

Thelma walks into the room, with water handing it to Chanel and Tyler. "Baby girl, do you mind? The driver will be here soon," she stated.

"Right, I almost forgot," Val stood hoping Chanel and Tyler do the same, without her having to say anything. "I'm sorry, guys; I have a driver coming over shortly to transport some items."

"No worries, I'm so glad we got a chance to meet. I know it means a lot to Tyler. I have a few rounds to make, before I head over to my mother's."

Val walked them to the door and stood outside embracing them. They stood still about ten more minutes admiring each other, as Tyler headed to get in the car. Chanel seemed stuck between leaving and actually moving. Val had to get back inside. Chanel was talking, but Val was admiring a car parked across the street. She wasn't sure if someone was sitting in there or not, like someone was leaning back in the seat. It made her uneasy and paranoid, so she was trying to get back in the house.

Just as she went in to hug Chanel, a gentleman out of nowhere emerged from the bushes.

"Chanel, Val, What the hell is going on?" the guy said, walking towards them, who happen to be Bird.

They both were stunned, looking at each other afraid for their lives. "Bird, what are you doing here?" Val asked loudly, hoping someone heard her.

"I actually came to talk to you, but I see you've been in touch with the enemy!"

Val just knew that entire situation was about to get crazy. Her and Chanel were scared out of their minds, and poor Tyler was sitting in the car with his headphones on, not paying attention. Val's gun was inside the house, she didn't know if Bird came to her in peace or what.

"I like this little reunion. Chanel where the hell is my son?"

Frightened Chanel stuttered, trying to speak. No one understood a word she said. "At my mom's."

WHO IS HE TO YOU?

Bird reached in his pockets and both ladies fell to the ground. They looked up at Bird, who only pulled out a piece of gum. "I'm here in peace ladies.

CHAPTER TWENTY-EIGHT

The Reunion

B ird reached for Val's hand, who was terrified to face him. She hesitated at first but reached out.

"Please can we talk? I really would like to get some things off my chest," he said. I know I'm not supposed to be here, but please just give me five minutes of your time, Val, and I'll never bother you again!"

Val looked over at Chanel, who was shaking her head no. Bird caught on and from the look he gave her, she curled up like a baby. It was the most frightening situation ever. Neither knew what to do.

"Bird, right now is not the time. I got family in the house and if they see you, they will call the police. Maybe we can get together and talk later?"

"Sure. So, you won't be a no show? I mean, this was the only way to get your attention. I tried the grocery store, that didn't work and sitting outside your place every night for that joker to be laid up with you. Right now is the perfect time!" he barked.

To know he's been outside watching Val's house was very disturbing, she didn't know what to think, that was sickening. What if she was taking out the trash or something happened to Bret? She wouldn't know what to do. She tried to come up with every excuse and a way to get in the house. Then there was Tyler, looking over at the scene trying to figure out what was going on, after Chanel said he was at her mom's.

"So are we going to talk or not, Val? Chanel, I'll deal with you later."

"Can I leave?" she asked.

"Sure, I just want to see my son. You on the other hand, are already dead to me!" he stated.

Chanel didn't know how long he'd been sitting outside of Val's place, or he would have seen them pull up and Tyler with her. She was trying her best to get up to get to her car in hopes of Tyler not being seen.

"Val, will you be okay? I really have to run," she said hoping Val got the hint. She had to get Tyler out of there but didn't want to leave her alone.

"Sure, you go ahead," she managed to get out.

Just as Chanel stood to leave, Thelma peeped out the door and Tyler managed to get out the car. "Baby, get back in the car. Hurry, let's go!" Chanel ordered.

"Oh no, Sabrina!" Thelma called out. She ran out onto the lawn, as Val stood to make her way in the house, just as Bird ran after Chanel pushing her to the ground.

"Bird!" Val turned around and screamed in agony as Tyler looked on.

"You lying bitch! My son been in the car all this time and you still lying to me, telling me he's at your mom's. I ought to kill you!" he hollered.

"Leave my mom alone!" Tyler yelled, running over to Chanel.

"Son, wait, please let me look at you," Bird pleaded. He grabbed Tyler and forced a hug on him, as tears ran down his face. "You have no idea how much I've missed you. I'm your father." Bird then stepped back, taken aback by Tyler's features. Tyler disconnected from him, concerned about his mother, and then pushed Bird away.

"A man that puts his hands on a woman, is no father to me!" Tyler emphasized. "Get away from me and my mother!" he hollered.

"But son, you don't understand. That bitch took you away from me!" Bird growled.

Val stepped closer to Bird as she saw the hurt in his eyes. He was rocking back and forth, admiring Tyler with hatred in his eyes for Chanel. By that time, Sabrina had run to the door, in fear.

"Val!" she called out.

"I'm okay Sabrina, please go back in the house."

Everyone was standing still in silence, fearing Bird's next move. Chanel managed to get up, as she grabbed her son. Bird walked behind her as Val looked back and forth. She mumbled for Sabrina to get help. She was scared out of her mind.

"You're not leaving here again with my son!"

"Bird or whatever your name is. I'm not going anywhere with you. I don't have a father!" Tyler shouted.

"You little punk bitch! I am your father and you will not talk to me like that. Get your ass over here, you are going with me!" Bird ordered.

Chanel managed to get in the car, while Tyler got in as well. Bird busted the window and glass shattered everywhere. He unlocked the door and pulled Chanel by her hair out of –the car. Val ran over to them and jumped on Bird's back, trying to stop him from hurting her.

"Bird, please leave, the police are on their way!" Sabrina called out. There were a few neighbors who heard the commotion and stood out to see what was going on.

"Val, please get off of me!" Bird demanded. He managed to drag Chanel onto the lawn and kick her. Val was still hanging onto his back, choking him at one point. *Whack!* He elbowed her, hitting her in the chest, knocking her to the ground. He then turned his attention to Val, "I came here in peace! Don't you ever grab me, you know I will break your jaw woman! You do remember what happened to your ass the last time, right? You want another beating?" Bird threatened.

WHO IS HE TO YOU?

Thelma and Sabrina ran out, just as Bird pulled out a gun. "Bird, please don't, it's not worth it!" Val cried.

"I should blow both of your brains out!" He then stood over Val, "Where is that nigga? Your little boyfriend is going to be a dead man when I see him!"

"Bird, Bret has nothing to do with any of this. What is it to you?"

"You bitch! You are my prize possession, that's what it is to me!" he shot back, with a look in his eyes that Val had never seen before.

Chanel and Tyler were trembling. Bird pointed the gun at Chanel and laughed. He was delusional. He was spinning out of control. "Look who's scared now, got my punk ass son the same way."

"Bird, I'm sorry!" Chanel uttered. "I had to take him away, this right here is toxic. You've got a problem!"

He shot into the windshield of the car. "Say that shit again!" he said as he walked towards her. Once he stood in front of Chanel, he laughed. He spat in her face. She wiped the saliva, as he then hit her with the gun,

Chanel was hurting, as people ran over and stopped dead in their tracks noticing Bird with the gun.

"Take another step, brother and that'll be your last walk," he ordered to a gentleman coming over to help. He then turned his attention to Tyler, "Son, I said come here!" he ordered.

"Please, let me get my bag out the car and we can leave," Tyler pleaded.

"No, no, no!" Chanel uttered.

Tyler quickly opened the car door to grab his bag and headset. Val wanted to rush him into the house without both of them getting killed so bad. Tyler slowly closed the door and stepped back. Val noticed something in his other hand and her mouth flew open. "Dad, I'm ready," he called out.

Bird had his gun in his right hand. Once Tyler came around the front of the car, he pulls out a gun and shoots. Bird immediately falls to the ground. Before Bird could lift his arm, his gun falls out. People started running over, as Tyler shoots again and again. His gun finally drops and he falls to the ground in tears.

"Baby, no!" Chanel hollered, as her son shot his father. Bird was shot three times, at least. Blood was everywhere. Tyler was hyperventilating, hysterical and scared. Everyone was grateful it happened, but not like that.

Val ran over to Tyler to console him as she heard Bret in the background. On lookers were terrified and disturbed at what just happened in their neighborhood.

"Val, where are you?" Bret called out in a panic. Val was speechless, as she noticed Bret looking over Bird's bloody body.

"Baby I'm right here," she replied.

He ran to her aid, trying to understand what took place. Val cried, as Thelma and Sabrina ran over. By that time, Lance ran overlooking for Sabrina.

"Babe the ambulance and police are here. Let's get everyone inside the house to calm down," Bret stated.

Thelma hugged her daughter and grabbed her by her face, "Sweetheart it's over now, Bird won't ever hurt you again!" she said in tears, "Oh my, God. I can't believe what just happened!" she shouted.

Bret and Lance helped Chanel and a weeping Tyler inside the house as Bird's lifeless body lay out on the concrete as blood rolled down the street, a scene Val will never forget. She wanted so desperately for him to change. Her love for him would eventually fade, but at that moment she still couldn't help wanting to cradle his bloody body in her arms.

Sabrina grabbed her arm as she stared at Bird's body. "It's over. I knew it would eventually end up this way, but never in a million years did I think his son would end up being the one to pull the trigger."

Val looked over at Sabrina and wept. "I just don't understand. He had so much going for himself."

"And you'll never understand. Let's go inside, the police are waiting."

Once Val got inside, the room looked dark. Bret and Lance were consoling Tyler and he talked about going to jail. There were several witnesses, who will make sure Tyler doesn't go anywhere.

"Chanel, I'm so sorry this happened," Val managed to say.

"Don't be, it's over now. I can stop running and you can finally enjoy life."

WHO IS HE TO YOU?

As the detective talked, Val's head started spinning. Her life started flashing before her eyes. Val's eyes were weakening and her body shook like no other. Before she knew it, she collapsed on the living room floor, as everyone ran to her aid, while the paramedics where outside tending to Bird. She heard voices, but her body just wouldn't respond.

THE AFTERMATH

A few weeks had passed and Val and Bret were finally settled into their place. She went through a lot the last few weeks dealing with the outcome of Bird's death. With all the witnesses, Bird's history of domestic violence and not staying away from Val, everything was in self-defense. The guilt of Tyler shooting his father was really weighing on him. Chanel had gotten him some really good help through counseling to help them both cope. She decided to move back to Georgia to be with her mom and family, so that was great.

Bird's mom, had his remains cremated. They weren't in the best place at the time of his death, so she decided his ashes would keep him close to her. Val's fallout after the incident had a lot to do with hyperventilation, where she started to panic and breathing too quickly. Her blood pressure had gotten too low. Seeing her ex shot and lying in a puddle of blood was something she never imagined. So she could only imagine how Tyler was feeling. The first week after it happened, Val was waking up every hour out of her sleep in a panic, which prompted Bret to take her to a doctor to get some help, so she could sleep.

Val sat on the edge of the bed looking out the window. There was a stream that flowed to the other side of the neighborhood from the back of the house. It was therapeutic to her, reminded Val of a place her father used to take her and Shai when they were little. She heard Bret in the kitchen brewing coffee. They were still dealing with their issues of trust. Bret didn't understand why Val didn't tell him she was in touch with Chanel, he once again felt like she was keeping things from him. Val wanted to tell him but thought everything would work itself out and blow over. She guessed it had to happen the way it did, in order for them to move on with their lives.

She heard Bret walking towards the bedroom and continued to stare out the window.

He peeped in the door, "Sweetheart, would you like anything to eat?"

"No, babe, I'm okay. I'll eat something later."

"Val, you really have to eat something. Eating here and there isn't healthy."

He walked in, creeping up behind her, and then wrapped his arms around her. Bret knew she was hurting and he wasn't helping the cause. He really loved Val and he would have understood more if she would confide in him.

"Babe, I think we need to get away for a few days. I think it would do us both some good," he stated. He turned Val around to face him, as he caressed her face. "I'm sorry and I know, I'm not helping, but Bird can't hurt you anymore. Sweetheart, it's time for you to live."

Tears were slowly running down Val's face. She knew Bret was right but didn't understand why she was feeling the way she was feeling. "I know, baby I'm so sorry," Val cried out. She was starting to beat herself up over what happened, but Bret wasn't having it.

"Stop it, Stop it! Nothing is your fault! Look at me, Val. Nothing is your fault..." he responded. He took Val's hand and placed it on his face. "Let's go get married."

Val looked at him like he was crazy and joking. "Come again?"

"Let's go get married, I mean it!" He pulled out a box from his sweats and her eyes lit up.

WHO IS HE TO YOU?

Val's tears turned into tears of joy. "Are you serious?"

"I was planning to do this later, but the timing is perfect. Will you marry me, Valerie Taylor?" He pulled out the ring, which was a round baguette white gold ring, the most beautiful ring she has ever seen. She didn't care about the carats, only her happiness at this stage in her life. He began to place the ring on her finger.

"Yes, I will marry you! Yes, yes, yes!" Val said in excitement. Bret had never seen the smile Val was wearing on her face before. She leaned in and kissed him long and hard.

Bret released himself from Val's grip. "We can continue this in Paris. Breakfast is waiting on you and we have to be at the airport in a few hours."

"Say what!" She didn't know how she was going to get it together in a few hours.

"Trust me, everything is in place, all you have to do is pack. We have engagement photos in place and a host of other things," he winked and walked out the room.

Val fell back on the bed; she was ecstatic. She had never felt that type of love before in her life and to know she was getting married had her on cloud nine. She needed to call her mom, sister, and Sabrina, but figured they already knew. She jumped up from the bed and took her little happy ass in the kitchen, where Paris awaited her.

"Oh my God! You are full of surprises!" Bret had the kitchen turned into a Paris theme. It was everything.

He handed her a menu and a Paris coffee mug filled with her usual, "Bonjour."

They toast. "A reason, why I love you so much."

"Également," he responded in French.

THE END

NATIONAL DOMESTIC VIOLENCE HOTLINE:
24/7 CALL SERVICES
CALL - 1-800-799-SAFE (7233), available 24/7

I don't know who needs to hear this, but you didn't deserve the abuse you endured. Abuse is never okay.

What Is Domestic Violence?

Does your partner ever....

> Insult, demean or embarrass you with put-downs?

> Control what you do, who you talk to or where you go?

> Look at you or act in ways that scare you?

> Push you, slap you, choke you or hit you?

> Stop you from seeing your friends or family members?

> Control the money in the relationship? Take your money or Social Security check.

> Make you ask for money or refuse to give you money?

> Make all of the decisions without your input or consideration of your needs?

> Tell you that you're a bad parent or threaten to take away your children?

> Prevent you from working or attending school?

> Act like the abuse is no big deal, deny the abuse or tell you it's your own fault?

WHO IS HE TO YOU?

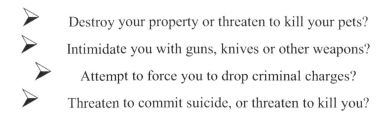

➤ Destroy your property or threaten to kill your pets?

➤ Intimidate you with guns, knives or other weapons?

➤ Attempt to force you to drop criminal charges?

➤ Threaten to commit suicide, or threaten to kill you?

If you answered 'yes' to even one of these questions, you may be in an unhealthy or abusive relationship.

SUBSCRIBE TO
BIANCA'S MAILING LIST

Stay updated with the author on new releases, giveaways, out and about, and much more!

www.authorbiancaharrison.com

OTHER BOOKS by BIANCA HARRISON

Someone To Call My Own

Forever His Wife

Inseparable

Deliver Me From Temptation

Deliver Me From Temptation 2

All books can be found on the Author Amazon Page
amazon.com/author/biancaharrison

Follow the Author:

https://www.facebook.com/authorbiancaharrison

https://twitter.com/mrsjanielle

Instagram/mrsjanielle

Snapchat/mrsjanielle

WHO IS HE TO YOU?

Made in the USA
Columbia, SC
18 September 2020